A
Harlequin
Romance

OTHER
Harlequin Romances
by REBECCA STRATTON

Many of these titles are available at your local bookseller, or through the Harlequin Reader Service.

For a free catalogue listing all available Harlequin Romances, send your name and address to:

HARLEQUIN READER SERVICE,
M.P.O. Box 707, Niagara Falls, N.Y. 14302
Canadian address: Stratford, Ontario, Canada N5A 6W4

or use order coupon at back of book.

THE GODDESS OF MAVISU

by

REBECCA STRATTON

Harlequin Books

TORONTO • LONDON • NEW YORK • AMSTERDAM • SYDNEY • WINNIPEG

Original hardcover edition published in 1975
by Mills & Boon Limited

SBN 373-01976-9

Harlequin edition published May, 1976

Printed In U.S.A.

CHAPTER ONE

DELIA leaned back against the rough trunk of a cypress and gazed up at the deep purple sky, scattered with stars like diamonds on velvet. Only a few kilometres away and on a slightly lower level the lights of Antalya vied with the stars, glittering and bright and lending a shimmering haze of gold to the night sky.

The sound of the sea reached her as little more than a whisper, barely audible above the movement of the cypress plumes that stirred in the warm night breeze, and behind her she could hear voices. Not loud voices, just the quiet conversation of her uncle and Clifford as they went over the day's finds by lamplight, unable to leave the site as the local hired workers had long since done.

As always Uncle Arthur's only interest lay with past centuries, back in the days when the Greeks had occupied this beautiful country and left their culture to become part of the exciting history of Turkey. Delia enjoyed archaeology, she would not have been persuaded to join the expedition otherwise, but she was more easily influenced by present conditions than by history.

Certainly those ancient Greeks had discovered a

paradise in Anatolia, especially along this exquisite coast with its turquoise blue waters and coral red cliffs festooned with tumbling waters. Delia had fallen in love with Anatolia at first sight and with Antalya and its vicinity in particular, but she was much more concerned about the present rather disturbing inhabitants than with the ancient Greeks. With one of them in particular.

Delia knew quite well, although her uncle and Clifford pooh-poohed the idea, that Kemal Selim disliked having them there at Mavisu, and she wished her uncle's enthusiasm for his calling had not led him to intrude on to private land in his pursuit of further knowledge.

Years ago her uncle, Professor Arthur Crompton, had known Sadi Selim, and when he heard that there might be some so far undiscovered Grecian remains on the old man's land he had immediately requested permission to start digging there so that he might prove or disprove the theory.

Sadi Selim had consented, apparently quite readily, but his grandson had made it plain more than once that he did not agree with the decision and resented the intrusion. In all honesty Delia was bound to sympathise with his feelings to some extent, for Mavisu was beautiful, and although their dig was small as yet and still concealed by a profusion of shrubs and trees their being there at all must have constituted an intrusion.

The whole of this Turquoise Coast was a treasure house of archaeology, of course, but new discoveries were always exciting and she was bound to sympathise with her uncle's point of view as well, for he was a man who thought of little else but his profession. Delia's father had been an enthusiastic amateur, but Arthur, his brother, was completely dedicated. As soon as Sadi Selim's permission was forthcoming he had sought official sanction and then organised a flight out with Delia and his assistant, Clifford Aitkin. Other necessary labour was recruited from among the local men.

Clifford Aitkin had been with her uncle ever since he left university and it had been his suggestion that Delia might like to come along as a lay helper. The suggestion had not been without another motive, Delia knew that, for she was well aware that Clifford was becoming increasingly interested in her personally, although her uncle had not so far realised it.

Clifford was a quiet, not quite shy man, and so far he had said nothing to her that could be construed as an approach, however tentative, but Delia had seen a look in his eyes that told her how things were going and she was not altogether averse to the idea. Clifford was quite attractive in a quiet and studious sort of way, but she always felt that he was so much older than she was, although he was no more than twenty-six, only five years older.

Delia sighed as she looked up again at the stars, then glanced over her shoulder to where a lamp burned dimly in the tent that housed their equipment and their finds. The three of them, her uncle, herself and Clifford, were guests in Sadi Selim's home, he had insisted on it, but while his hospitality was gracious and generous there was always his grandson's attitude to contend with.

It was time they went back to the house if they were to be ready in time for dinner, although Uncle Arthur would dislike having to leave his precious specimens, he always did. She must insist on their being in time, for she could not face another embarrassment such as occurred last week when they had been unforgivably late for dinner simply because her uncle could not be dragged away from his treasures.

Delia could have gone to dinner alone, of course, but she was much too nervous to sit at table without her uncle, especially with Kemal Selim's dark discouraging eyes on her. Madame Renoir was kindness itself, but then she was not the head of the house, nor did she share her nephew's dislike of the English visitors.

Another glance at her wristwatch warned her that she dared not leave her reminder any longer, and she eased herself away from the support of the tree and started across to the tent, but as she made her way through the scented mass of shrubs and trees that surrounded their dig someone stepped into her path.

She drew a sharp, almost audible breath and put a hand to her throat, her eyes wide and shiningly bright in the soft light as she shrank back in her brief alarm against the cool scented mass of a magnolia. The moonlight merely suggested the red-gold of her hair and her eyes looked as dark as night instead of their natural green when she looked up at him.

'Miss Crompton.' He stood outlined against the pale pink tamarisk blossom, his height exaggerated by the conditions, and seeming to tower over her.

Kemal Selim was tall, taller than either Clifford or her uncle, and in the present lighting he looked even darker than usual too. His hair looked jet black when in reality it was a very dark brown and his eyes were not the glittering jet they appeared at the moment but a deep glowing brown, set in short, thick lashes that emphasised both their depth and their colour.

To all appearances he was Turkish, for his looks owed very little to his French mother, and Delia suspected he preferred it so. He was a disconcerting man in every way, both in his looks and in his manner. His features were strong and hawkish, much more suggestive of the East than of Western Europe, with straight dark brows and high cheek-bones, while his manner, particularly with Delia, had the proud arrogance of an old-time Pasha. He was about thirty-two or three years old and still un-married—and Delia often wondered why.

He looked at her, having spoken her name, and she blinked a little anxiously as her heart thudded alarmingly against her ribs. Not only had he startled her but his appearance always had the most dis-comfiting effect on her, no matter how much she tried to pretend otherwise.

'I—I didn't see you,' she told him. 'You startled me.'

He ignored her complaint, made no apology for startling her, but glanced over at the tent where her uncle's voice could be heard, now higher pitched as his enthusiasm for his treasures grew. A section of stone capital from the body of a temple was enough to send him wild with delight, and Delia at least could understand his enthusiasm.

'Professor Crompton has had some success, *hanim*?' Kemal Selim asked, and something in his voice combined with the arching of one dark brow brought a swift flush to Delia's cheeks.

'We've done quite well today,' she told him, unable to do anything about the edge of defensiveness on her voice. 'Beside a section of capital we found a piece of what could be a carved frieze, so it looks as if there *was* a temple here. Naturally Uncle Arthur's very excited about it—we all are.'

'Of course!' Again his tone made her frown, but she merely thrust out her small rounded chin and refused to be angry about it. 'I imagine you were about to remind your colleagues that it is almost time for dinner,' he said, and the implication was unmistakable.

His English was impeccable, Delia could find no fault with it at all, but she always felt he was talking down to her, as if she were some kind of inferior being that he only tolerated. Possibly it had something to do with the traditional attitude of the Turk towards women, although Sadi Selim, his grandfather, was never less than courteous and charming.

'We won't be late, Mr. Selim,' she promised in a cool voice, and once again that dark brow elevated swiftly to the dark fall of hair across his forehead.

Half expecting him to make some comment on their disastrously late entrance last week, Delia waited, ready to leap to her uncle's defence, but instead Kemal Selim looked down at her steadily for a second before he spoke. 'You do not share the enthusiasm of your uncle for history, *hanim*?' he asked, and Delia stared at him in surprise for a moment.

His interest was unexpected and disconcerting and she wondered at the reason for it. He was a man she could never feel at ease with and it therefore took her several moments to find an answer. He always called her the very formal and impersonal *hanim* without the addition of her first name as his grandfather did, or else Miss Crompton, which was scarcely more friendly.

The white dinner jacket he wore somehow served only to add to the earthy, primitive cast of his features, and she recognised him suddenly as a stunningly attractive man, albeit a dangerous one. Hastily bringing her hammering pulse under control, she glanced again over her shoulder where her uncle's gauntly thin shadow was cast against the flimsy tent by the lamplight.

'Oh yes, I'm very interested,' she said, 'but to Uncle Arthur—well, archaeology is his whole life. It means so much more to him than to an amateur like me.'

'And Mr. Aitkin?' The dark eyes still looked down at her steadily, bringing a fresh urgency to her heart's beat. 'Is he fired with the same daunt-

11

less enthusiasm as the professor?' Swiftly the eyes swept over her in a gaze that brought a bright flush to her cheeks. 'Or has he other interests, *hanim*?' he added, and it was impossible to mistake his meaning.

There was something challenging and infinitely disturbing about the way he was looking at her, and Delia swallowed hastily on a sudden brief sense of panic as she faced him. The magnolia's scent surrounded her, enveloped her, as she stood embraced by its branches, and the other scents and sounds of the garden too had an effect that was almost intoxicating.

The pale tamarisk blossoms that threw the tall arrogance of Kemal Selim into relief and the whispering plumes of the cypress trees stirred by the warm breeze off the sea, even that rich, diamond-studded sky with its silver moon, seemed unreal, and she felt strangely lightheaded, as if it was all part of some exotic dream she was bound to wake from soon.

'You do not answer,' Kemal Selim reminded her quietly, breaking into her dream. 'Can it be that you do not know?'

Delia took a short step forward, away from the cool touch of the magnolia leaves, and shook her head. 'I can't answer for Mr. Aitkin,' she said in a voice that trembled despite her attempts to control it. 'And if you'll excuse me, Mr. Selim——'

'Of course!'

He made no attempt to step out of her way, and to reach the tent where her uncle and Clifford were she must pass between him and the spread of a huge pink azalea. She made herself as small as possible and even turned sideways on, but for all that the limited space made it impossible for her not to come in contact with him.

Her body was pressed against him only briefly, but it was long enough for her to sense the muscular strength of him through his jacket and she flinched as if she had been burned. It was the first time she had been in actual physical contact with him and the effect was more devastating than anything she could have anticipated. Glancing up, she found the dark eyes fixed on her steadily, enigmatic and fathomless in the dim light.

'*Affedersiniz, hanim,*' he apologised, but Delia hurried away without being really sure if a brief glimpse of white teeth was really a smile or not.

Dinner at Mavisu had been a revelation to Delia, although by now she was growing accustomed to the lavishness of Turkish hospitality. Exotic dishes followed one another in seemingly endless variety and were accompanied by glasses of *raki*, a spirit that Delia felt was very much an acquired taste, although her uncle and Clifford seemed to find it palatable enough.

Unable to do full justice to these gargantuan feasts, Delia was aware that Kemal Selim noticed each time she bypassed one of the dishes because she simply could not cope with the quantities, and she sometimes wondered uneasily if she was committing a breach of good manners by refusing them.

The setting for these nightly feasts was as exotic as the food and Delia always felt as if she had stepped into the past whenever she sat down amid the splendours of the dining salon. Sadi Selim, a traditionalist at heart, had Westernised his household to the extent of using a dining table and chairs, but the beautiful carpets, bronze filigree lamps and bowls of scented water were all so much part of tradition that Delia believed it was the reason her uncle felt so much at home there.

She looked at him now, a swift, surreptitious look below half lowered lids, and saw him deep in conversation with his host. His thin bony shape was clad in an old-fashioned dinner jacket that looked at least one size too large for him and he looked as out of place in that as he did in most of his clothes, his large head with its prematurely grey hair inclined attentively towards his host. Uncle Arthur spoke passable Turkish, but he was much too tactful to use it when Sadi Selim had such an excellent command of English.

Sadi Selim was everything Delia had expected in a powerful and wealthy man, except that he was much less inclined to be autocratic than his grandson was, and he very obviously enjoyed her uncle's company. He was a big man by any standards, and his years had done little to distort his bearing; he looked little older than her uncle, although he must have had the advantage of thirty years or so. His black hair was only streaked with grey and the strong hawklike features inherited by his grandson were as bold as ever, though smiling seemed to come easily to him.

Opposite to her, across the table, Clifford seemed to be following the conversation of the two older men but saying little, his grey eyes behind their wide horn-rims glinting with interest. He was no taller than her uncle but more sturdily built, and his rather delicate features suggested that he was both less dedicated and less self-confident than his mentor. An attractive man but a dreamer, and one whom Delia could well imagine Kemal Selim would despise.

Instinctively her eyes turned to the place at their host's right hand and she felt that same curious flutter of reaction she always did whenever she looked at Kemal Selim. It was almost as if each time was the first time she had set eyes on him and there was always an element of surprise when she realised how stunningly attractive he was and how blatantly sensual. As if he sensed her interest the dark eyes held her gaze boldly and she felt a warm flush of colour in her cheeks as she hastily looked away.

His aunt, Madame Renoir, sat next to her at the other end of the table, the two women side by side, as if their presence there at all was merely a concession to Western standards. Sadi Selim, for all his charming manners, was still a traditionalist at heart.

'You have made progress today, *ma chère*?' Madame Renoir asked, and Delia smiled and nodded.

'Quite a lot, *madame*,' she said. 'It's pretty certain now that there *was* a temple here, and that's very exciting.'

Madame smiled, making a grimace that expressed her opinion plainly enough. 'So,' she said, 'there is evidence of an ancient goddess in our midst, huh?'

'It seems almost certain,' Delia agreed, and Madame Renoir looked at her with a glint of mischief in her eyes, nodding her head as she leaned forward confidentially.

'But I am sure our two young men were well aware of that without excavating for ruins, *ma chère!*' she murmured, and her expression left little doubt as to her meaning so that Delia glanced hastily and warily at Kemal Selim, thankful that he had not overheard. 'You are a very lovely young girl,' Madame Renoir went on undeterred, 'and what young man does not prefer that his goddesses have flesh and blood, eh?'

Delia said nothing but merely smiled, for it was doubtful if either of the two young men referred to saw her as a goddess, certainly not Kemal Selim, to whom she could have been no more than an unwelcome guest in his grandfather's home.

But she did not take offence, for she liked the little Frenchwoman and found her easy to talk to and very ready to be friendly. Despite having spent more than thirty years in Turkey she still delved into her own tongue quite often, and especially for terms of endearment. She was short and stockily built with greying brown hair and light brown eyes, and she had a rather impish sense of humour which Delia felt sure must have been little exercised during her years of exile.

Madame Renoir's sister had married Sadi Selim's only son during the second world war and they had both been killed, along with her own husband, when Kemal was still a babe in arms. As soon as she was able to travel freely she had brought to Sadi Selim his only grandson and the hospitality he had offered her in gratitude had persuaded her to stay on.

She had cared for Kemal with as much devotion as if he had been her own son, even though she had seen him grow into a man as completely Turkish as his father and his grandfather were. She seemed to have no regrets about her long sojourn in an alien land, and indeed she fitted into this very Turkish household perfectly and seemed very happy.

As she looked at Delia her brown eyes sparkled. 'You like to—dig?' she asked, as if such an occupation was beyond her comprehension. 'Do you really enjoy it, *ma chère*?'

Delia laughed, shaking her head to deny any serious participation in the actual excavating. 'I mostly just keep the records, *madame*,' she said, 'that's why I'm here. Sometimes I'm allowed to actually help uncover the finds, but to be perfectly honest, I'm not very good at it.'

'Ah!' Madame Renoir smiled her understanding, but it was obvious that the appeal and fascination of archaeology was a closed book to her and she shrugged her ample shoulders in resignation. 'I would become very bored,' she said. 'Do you not long to see something more exciting than old ruins,

17

Delia?' She used her hands to try and convey her meaning. 'Would you not like to drive, perhaps, and to see some of the beauties of Anatolia?'

Unsure just how serious the question was, Delia took a moment to consider. She would like to see some of the countryside, she could not deny it. Perhaps even go shopping in Antalya or drive along the coast to Side or Alanya; there was so much to see and she only now realised how restricted her activities had been lately.

It had not occurred to Clifford to offer to take her driving and sightseeing, but she couldn't really blame him for that, her uncle was dedicated to his task and he expected the same singlemindedness in his assistant. It was not that Uncle Arthur would have no sympathy with the idea of Clifford taking her out somewhere occasionally, but it simply did not occur to him that anyone would want to do anything else, and Clifford was not bold enough to suggest it even if he thought of it.

'I—I'd enjoy going out somewhere for a change,' Delia said, and realised as she made the admission that Kemal Selim was looking at her with obvious interest.

'Then we will go!' Madame Renoir decided with a smile. 'And since your uncle and Monsieur Aitkin are occupied with the digging, I think that Kemal will drive you and me for a tour of the sights, eh?' She looked along the table at her nephew, her eyes twinkling merrily. 'Will you not, *chéri*?' she asked.

Delia hastily avoided the steady gaze of those dark eyes, her breath caught in her throat. The company of Kemal Selim was something she had not counted on and she doubted very much if he would be as amenable as his aunt suggested. Either way would prove a source of embarrassment to Delia, she felt sure of it.

'If Miss Crompton agrees to the arrangement,' Kemal Selim answered quietly, but without hesitation. 'Do you, *hanim*?'

Delia scarcely believed her own ears and she hesitated, though only briefly. She was aware suddenly that Clifford had apparently abandoned his interest in the conversation between her uncle and their host and was looking across at her with a faint frown between his brows, as if he was unsure what was being said but suspected it was not to his liking.

Her heart was thudding heavily in her breast and Delia found the prospect of being taken sightseeing by Kemal Selim much more exciting than she could have imagined, even with Madame Renoir to chaperone them. 'Of course—I'll be very grateful if you can spare the time, Mr. Selim, thank you,' she said in a not quite steady voice, and he inclined his head in a brief gesture that somehow mocked her thanks.

'*Bir sey degil, hanim!*' He murmured the words softly, but even so her uncle looked across at him curiously. Meeting his gaze, Kemal smiled faintly. 'I am to take your niece for a drive, professor,' he told him. 'With your permission, of course, and in the company of *madame*, my aunt.'

'Oh!' For a few seconds the professor looked

vaguely startled, as if he had suddenly been pitched into an alien world. 'A drive, you say? Oh yes, of course, Kemal Bey, that's very kind of you!' He turned his short-sighted eyes on Delia again and smiled. 'You go and enjoy yourself, Delia my dear,' he told her. 'There are some magnificent sites all along this coast. The—the theatre at Aspendos, you must see that, and the city at Perge. They're both only a few kilometres from here and you'd find them most interesting!'

To Delia it was no more than she expected and she barely restrained a smile. It was useless to expect her uncle to show an interest in anything other than archaeological ruins, but Madame Renoir was shaking her head at him in gentle despair. 'No, no, *monsieur*,' she chided. 'It is to make a change for Delia that we wish to take her driving. Some shopping perhaps, or to visit the beaches and swim —there is much to see and do.' Her bright, mischievous eyes turned again to Delia. 'You would like to swim, eh, *chérie*?'

'Oh yes, I'd love to!' Delia said, and Madame Renoir nodded her satisfaction.

'It is agreed,' she declared firmly. 'Tomorrow we will go!'

Delia looked at her uncle almost apologetically. He would be at a loss to understand why she wanted to get away for a while and see something more of Turkey than the limited confines of Sadi Selim's property, no matter how beautiful it was. The need for outside distractions would not make sense to him when they were daily growing more close to proving a theory, and she felt almost guilty as she looked at him.

'I won't be gone very long, Uncle Arthur,' she told him. 'But I'd love to go shopping with Madame Renoir, and go swimming as well, if it's possible.'

'It is possible,' Kemal Selim interposed quietly, 'and I am a strong swimmer, *hanim*, you need have no fears.'

'Oh! Oh no, of course—I haven't!'

Delia curled her hands tightly into themselves. The possibility of such personal attention had never even entered her head and she found her heart racing wildly when she contemplated the idea of that strong, lean body swimming beside her in the warm sea. Even in imagination it was a dizzying thought and she hastily shook herself back to common sense before her emotions got out of hand.

'Lara is little more than twenty kilometres from here,' Kemal Selim was saying, and his strong hands dismissed the distance as unimportant. 'It has an excellent beach and it will not be over-populated at this time of year.'

Meaning that there would be fewer intrusive foreign visitors, Delia thought ruefully, but refused to be tempted by the obvious bait. Hesitantly she met his eyes, quite incredibly excited at the prospect of going out with him. 'I'm sure it's lovely,' she said, 'and I'd love to go.'

Once more he inclined his head in that half mocking bow. 'Then you shall go, *hanim*!' he said.

Her uncle still looked vaguely puzzled by it all, but Madame Renoir was smiling, a wide beam of satisfaction that gave a glow to her brown eyes, and it was only as she resumed her meal that Delia noticed Clifford's frown. He had never before shown signs of jealousy, but she could think of no other explanation for that frown other than dislike of her going with Kemal Selim.

'If I'd known you wanted to go swimming, Delia,' he ventured in his quiet voice, 'I'd have taken you —why didn't you say?'

Uneasily aware that everyone at the table was waiting to hear what she had to say, although ostensibly getting on with their meal, Delia shook her head. 'I—I didn't like to bother you, Clifford,' she told him. 'You're so busy, you and Uncle Arthur, and I didn't like to take you away just when things are going well.'

Clifford's grey eyes studied her curiously for a second, as if he too found her desire for change beyond his understanding. 'Things *are* going well,' he agreed, 'that's why I can't understand why you suddenly want to go off somewhere, just when we've made a breakthrough!'

'Perhaps you grow tired of history, Delia Hanim,' Sadi Selim suggested quietly from the head of the table, and Delia hastily shook her head, seeking an answer that would be both truthful and polite.

'Oh no, not at all!' she denied, and smiled at the old man reassuringly. 'It's simply that I—I'd like to see more of your lovely country, Sadi Bey. I'm sure there's more to Turkey than one ruined temple!'

'Very much more,' Sadi Selim agreed, and nodded his head as if he recognised her tact and it pleased him. 'Also you will find my grandson an excellent instructor in many things, Delia Hanim. There is much you will discover about our country and our people under his guidance.'

It sounded, Delia thought a little dizzily, as if he anticipated her spending the rest of her stay in Kemal Selim's company, and she was quite sure that the younger man had neither the intention nor the desire for that. Glancing at Kemal briefly, she shook her head. 'Oh, but I couldn't put Kemal Bey to so much trouble too often,' she denied in a deceptively meek voice. 'I'm sure he has other and more important things to do.'

'And I can take you anywhere you want to go,' Clifford insisted, speaking up swiftly before Kemal had time to either agree with Delia or to support his grandfather's suggestion.

Her uncle, apparently following the general gist of the conversation, peered at Clifford over the top of his spectacles and frowned. 'Oh, I don't think so, my dear fellow,' he told him. 'We're getting on very well, but I need your help now more than ever when we're nearing our goal.' He looked at Delia with a vague, kindly smile on his face. 'Besides,' he added cheerfully, 'Delia doesn't need you to run around after her, do you, my dear?'

Between two stools, Delia looked at Clifford with sympathy and understanding. She would have liked to have his company, but she could not honestly claim that his not being there would spoil her enjoyment, whereas there was an exciting sense of

anticipation about Kemal Selim being her guide—
always providing he agreed, of course.

Quite unconsciously she glanced again at Kemal,
but he was getting on with his meal and apparently
not taking the slightest interest in what was being
said. 'Oh, I'll be all right, Uncle Arthur,' she
assured him, and was not quite fast enough to avoid
Kemal's eyes when he suddenly looked up.

'Naturally you will be—all right, *hanim*,' he told
her. 'Have I not given my word?'

CHAPTER TWO

MADAME RENOIR had had no second thoughts about
the promised outing, as Delia discovered the following morning just after breakfast. Her uncle and
Clifford had already left for the dig, although
Clifford had given her a backward glance as he
went out that she thought was meant to convey a
dislike of the situation—the same dislike he had
implied last evening at dinner.

The big *salon* with its countless mirrors and
brightly coloured hanging rugs was one of Delia's
favourite rooms and spelled the very essence of
Turkey, she thought. An ornately carved ceiling
and various brass and gilt ornaments made it
exotic, and wide open windows, their shutters

fastened back, let in a blessedly cool breeze from the not too distant ocean.

It was delightfully quiet and peaceful and Delia sat beside one of the windows looking out over the gardens, curled up on one of the huge traditional floor cushions, still unsure whether or not she looked forward to several hours in the company of Kemal Selim. His aunt had more or less commandeered his services as chauffeur and Sadi Selim had given him little option about acting as guide. Kemal himself had seemed willing enough, but Delia still had reservations about it.

Madame Renoir's appearance put an end to her speculation and she looked up hastily and smiled, then lazily got to her feet. Madame Renoir swept an approving glance over the light blue cotton dress she wore and nodded, apparently satisfied with her appearance, although Delia herself had wondered if it was not a little too simple for shopping in town.

'Charming,' Madame Renoir declared smilingly. 'You look quite charming, *ma chère*!'

'Thank you, *madame*.' Delia looked across the room, wondering where Kemal could be and if he had, after all, changed his mind.

'Kemal is fetching the car,' she was told, as if the older woman had followed her thoughts. 'We will see him in a few moments.'

She checked that Delia had sun-glasses and a shady hat against the sun, and that the large canvas bag she was taking contained a swimming costume and everything else she was likely to need. 'First we will visit Antalya and perhaps do some shopping,' she decided, 'and then we will find a good beach for you to have the swim, *ma chère*.' Her round face smiled and the bright brown eyes hinted mischief as she looked at Delia slyly. 'This day will be good for you and for Kemal too,' she decreed. 'You do not have the gift to—*re*lax, huh?'

A little startled to find herself classed with Kemal in any category at all, Delia smiled doubtfully. 'I can't answer for Kemal Bey,' she told her, 'but I'm perfectly relaxed, *madame*, and I'm certainly looking forward to our trip.'

'*Bon!*'

Leading the way into the wide coolness of the hall, Madame Renoir squeezed her hand impulsively, her brown eyes bright with anticipation, and for the first time Delia realised just how much it meant to the little Frenchwoman to have feminine company after living in an all-male household for several years.

Sadi Selim, she knew, had three daughters, but all were married now and had daughters of their own. Since his wife's death some years before the household had lacked feminine company altogether except for the servants and Madame Renoir must have missed it.

'Do you go shopping very often, *madame*?' Delia asked, and those expressive plump shoulders shrugged lightly.

'Whenever I wish to,' she said, then smiled as if she suddenly realised that Delia saw her as a lonely exile. 'But I have friends whom I visit, *ma chère*,' she told her softly. 'And this is my home—I am content.'

'Oh yes, of course!' Delia agreed hastily. 'I simply wondered if you ever——' She stopped, seeking the right words, and Madame Renoir smiled understanding as she shook her head.

'If I ever grow lonely?' she suggested. '*Mais non, petite*, my life is too full! Of course when Kemal takes a wife I will be happier, for then——' She shrugged those expressive shoulders once more and her eyes gleamed with anticipation for the moment. 'Perhaps I will be allowed to care for Kemal's little ones, hmm?'

'Oh! Oh yes, I'm sure you will!' Delia assured her hastily, stunned for the moment by the thought of Kemal being on the brink of marriage.

It was oddly discomfiting being drawn into such a conversation, and Delia found herself in something of a quandary. She was reluctant to appear any more than politely interested and yet she could not deny a consuming curiosity about the man she found at once disturbing and irresistible. She could not imagine why Madame Renoir had spoken so freely on so intimate a matter as her nephew's personal affairs, but Delia's pulses were suddenly hammering so hard that she felt breathless with it.

'But I'd no idea that Kemal was——' She stopped hastily, appalled to realise how close she had come to betraying the curiosity she felt about Kemal's plans, and seeing the warm flush of colour in her cheeks Madame Renoir smiled faintly and patted her hand.

'I too have no idea, *chérie,*' she confessed softly but with a hint of mischief in her eyes. 'But I am hopeful that soon my Kemal will gladden the heart of his grandpapa and also his aunt by taking a wife —*le bon Dieu* knows it is time that he did!'

Delia merely smiled, trying to make it appear as if the subject was of no more than passing interest to her, but she would have given much to discover whether or not Kemal Selim had some wealthy and beautiful Turkish girl in mind for the honour. That the chosen bride would be both wealthy and beautiful Delia had no doubt—Kemal Selim was the kind of man who would expect nothing less.

Shaking herself hastily out of a train of thought that she found strangely disturbing, she turned her head to see Clifford coming across the hall. Even at a distance his grey eyes behind their lenses looked darkly unhappy and she felt suddenly and quite inexplicably guilty about the proposed outing.

He was wearing a pair of well-washed fawn shorts and a faded blue shirt, a combination that did nothing to dispel the air of absentminded untidiness about him. A frown drew his brows together above the dark rims of his spectacles as he came across to where she stood beside Madame Renoir, and it struck her that he had something on his mind.

'I wondered if you might be gone by now, Delia,' he said, and flicked a brief uneasy glance at Madame Renoir, as if he wished she was anywhere but standing beside Delia at the moment.

More certain than ever that he had something on

his mind, Delia shook her head. 'Mr. Selim—Kemal Bey's gone for the car,' she told him. She was never sure whether she ought to anglicise Kemal's name or not, and Madame Renoir glanced at her curiously when she changed her mind. 'Is something wrong, Clifford?' she asked hastily. 'Did you want to see me about something?'

Clifford said nothing for a moment, but he puffed a thin stream of blue smoke from the pipe he held clamped between his teeth and it was obvious that she had been right to assume there was something on his mind, just as it was obvious that the presence of Madame Renoir deterred him from saying what it was.

It took the little Frenchwoman only a moment to realise that her being there was inhibiting his explanation and she smiled and raised one brow, glancing between the two of them archly. 'I will leave you to speak with Monsieur Aitkin, *ma chère*,' she told Delia. 'But Kemal will be here in just a moment, so do not linger too long, hmm?'

'Oh no, *madame*, of course not—I'll be ready!' They watched her as she walked across the wide hall and passed out into the sunshine and the lush gardens at the front of the house, then Delia turned again to Clifford, one brow raised curiously. '*Did* you want to say something to me, Clifford?' she asked, and he took a moment to answer.

It was obvious that he found whatever it was on his mind difficult to put into words, and she almost felt sorry for him. 'I don't quite know how to begin, Delia,' he confessed after a moment or two, and again he hesitated to go on.

Delia, keeping an anxious eye open for Kemal Selim's arrival with the car, hoped Clifford was not going to take so long coming to the point that she would find herself keeping Kemal waiting. The prospect of that did not appeal to her at all, particularly since he was probably taking her merely to oblige his aunt.

Looking at Clifford's rather dreamy features she felt a stab of impatience suddenly, then a moment later was appalled to think that she could have reacted so. 'I'm sorry, Clifford,' she told him, 'but Kemal Selim will be here at any minute with the car. Is it important? Couldn't it wait until I come back?'

Clifford's frown deepened, she thought, and wondered if it could be simply his concern for her being in the company of strangers that was bothering him. She knew he felt something for her, although nothing had ever been said or even hinted at, but his behaviour at the moment seemed to suggest that his feelings for her went much deeper than she had realised. His right hand was clamped so tightly about the bowl of the pipe that she expected the stem to snap at any moment under the pressure.

'Delia, don't you know how I feel? Didn't you know that I'd have taken you anywhere if only I'd known you wanted to go?' He sounded oddly breathless as the words came tumbling over one another. 'Why didn't you ask *me*? Why Selim? Couldn't you have mentioned that you were tired of the dig—bored with being in the same place?

I'd have taken you willingly!'

Delia took a moment to answer. She had not realised just how upset he was about her going with Kemal Selim and for a moment the knowledge stunned her. Obviously she had been a long way out in her understanding of his feelings.

'But I'm not in the least tired or bored,' she denied earnestly. 'And I'd certainly no intention of —of hurting your feelings, Clifford. It was just that when the chance arose to make a change—well, I took advantage of it, that's all.'

'Oh, Delia!' He took one of her hands and pressed his own thin strong fingers over hers. 'Why didn't you ask me?'

Delia considered for a moment. She could have mentioned it, but she hadn't simply because he seemed so totally committed to the work in hand and because she had not realised the possibilities until the way had been opened up for her by Madame Renoir's suggestion. She had certainly had no idea how she would be upsetting Clifford by accepting the invitation.

'I—I didn't think about it,' she told him after a moment or two. 'I honestly didn't think about going anywhere else until Madame Renoir suggested it, Clifford, and there's no need for you to feel— slighted at all. It's only a day's shopping and a swim in the sea, that's all!'

Clifford's grey eyes gazed at her earnestly for a moment and he said nothing, but his whole attitude spoke of a tension that concealed much stronger emotions than anything she would have suspected him of. 'It won't be all,' he argued with unexpected bitterness. 'There'll be other times, other outings! Madame Renoir has her own reasons for taking you on this trip!'

He puffed out more smoke and successfully concealed the expression on his face while Delia, genuinely puzzled, frowned at him curiously. 'I don't think I understand,' she told him, and Clifford looked suddenly uneasy, as if he feared he had said too much.

'Maybe I'm wrong,' he said slowly and with obvious reluctance, 'but the way I see it, Madame Renoir has plans for you that I definitely don't like!'

'Plans?' she frowned at him still, but her heart was thudding anxiously with the first suspicions of what he meant—suspicions that took her breath away. 'I—I think you're dramatising, Clifford,' she said in a voice that was not quite steady. 'What plans can Madame Renoir have that can possibly concern me?'

Once again Clifford took time to answer and Delia fretted with impatience. She could hear the sound of a car outside, which meant that Kemal Selim would be ready for her at any second now, and she simply could not go until she knew exactly what Clifford meant. Clifford too heard the engine stop and the slamming of a car door and he glanced hastily over his shoulder before turning back to her again.

'I think you know what I mean, Delia,' he told her. 'Both Sadi Selim and Madame Renoir want to see Kemal married, and Madame at least has no doubt who she wants for the role of bride to her precious nephew!'

'Clifford!'

She called after him, but Clifford was already half way to the doors, stunned by his own outspokenness, and Delia stared at his departing back with wide, bright eyes. Her heart was beating so hard that she felt breathless and it lurched crazily a second later when Kemal came in at the door. She almost felt she couldn't face him after the implications that Clifford had made, but she had little choice now that he was within touching distance, his dark eyes curious because he had heard her call out.

The two men barely acknowledged each other's presence, Clifford striding out into the sunshine, his thin figure stiff with embarrassment, and Kemal coming across to Delia unhesitatingly in the long easy strides that always reminded her of some big, dangerous animal. He looked down at her for a moment without speaking, his brown eyes flitting swiftly over her flushed face, then he arched one brow and looked at her enquiringly.

'Is there something wrong, *hanim*?' he asked coolly, and Delia shook her head.

'No,' she denied a little breathlessly. 'No, nothing's wrong.'

He regarded her for a moment as if he suspected she was lying, but then he inclined his head briefly and extended one hand towards the open doors. 'Then if you are ready,' he said, 'we are waiting!'

Suddenly more nervous than she had ever been of him, Delia stood her ground, her eyes downcast, searching her brain frantically for excuses, reasons for not going. 'I—if you'd rather not go, Mr. Selim,' she ventured after a moment or two, 'I don't mind, honestly. I mean,' she hastened to explain, 'I know you were more or less—forced to come on this outing and if you'd rather——'

She stopped short when a hand slid beneath her elbow and strong fingers curled over and into her soft flesh, urging her across the hall and towards the doors. 'I am not forced to do anything I have no wish to do, *hanim*,' he informed her coolly. 'That much you should know about me, at least!'

'I know,' Delia agreed, still trying to find reasons, 'but I thought——'

'Do not keep me waiting longer,' Kemal Selim said firmly, his hand under her elbow giving her no option but to go with him. 'I am not a patient man!'

'I know that too!' The retort was instinctive and for a moment Delia wondered if he would be angry enough to change his mind after all. Instead, when she glanced at him from the corner of her eyes, she caught a brief and quite unexpected glimpse of white teeth in the darkly tanned face and could scarcely believe he was smiling.

'Then waste no more time, *hanim*!' he told her firmly, and Delia went with him meekly out into the scented spring air, her hands clutching tightly on her handbag. How on earth, she wondered, was she going to cope with a whole day in Kemal

Selim's company, especially now that Clifford had put such disturbing ideas into her head?

'Antalya!' Madame Renoir said after what seemed like a remarkably short drive, and Delia gazed around her at the delightful suburbs of the town she had heard so much about but so far had not visited until now. It had seemed like a dream city, shimmering in the bright sun or vying with the stars at night with its lights perched among the night skies above the sea—now she could see that the reality was as enchanting as the dream.

The sunny streets were bordered with orange trees, and the purple blossom of bougainvillea grew riotously as borders and hedges, while wide shady plane trees offered less exotic but no less welcome shade. There was no shortage of water in this lush, fertile town either, its presence was both audible and visible everywhere that mountain streams surfaced in the city streets and were curbed and banked with grass and flowers and shaded by short, sturdy palm trees, as cool and beautiful as they were unexpected.

Antalya was built around a lovely bay, shimmering clear and a jewel-bright turquoise in colour, with streams of cool mountain water rushing down from the Taurus mountains behind the town and ending their journey in a spectacular display of tumbling falls from the cliffs' edge. The rocky coastline gave rise to incredible possibilities and the builders of Antalya had taken every advantage of it. Apart from its tiny harbour which lay at the foot of them most of Antalya itself was perched aloft on the steep, precipitous cliffs, a narrow and staggeringly twisty road allowing access to the harbour and the quay.

'It looks wonderful!' said Delia, and caught a brief but meaningful exchange of glances between Kemal and his aunt.

'Would you like to go shopping or look at Antalya?' Madame Renoir asked with a smile, and Delia had no hesitation in choosing the latter.

'There seems so much to see,' she explained, wondering as she spoke if Madame Renoir was disappointed in her choice. 'Do you mind very much if I go sightseeing, *madame*?' she asked. 'It all looks so lovely and I've never really seen a Turkish town.'

'But of course not, *chérie*!' Madame Renoir smiled at Kemal, one brow raised in question. 'You will not mind if Delia looks at the sights, will you, *cher* Kemal?'

'I am yours to command,' Kemal stated quietly, and flicked only a brief glance in Delia's direction, but it was enough to set her heart beating rapidly and to bring a faint flush of colour to her cheeks. 'But first we must park the car,' he went on, apparently oblivious of the effect he had. 'It is not possible to see Antalya properly from a car.'

'I'm sorry if I'm a nuisance,' Delia told him with a meekness that was not altogether assumed, and once more the dark eyes met hers for a moment before they returned to the road.

'Turkish hospitality is a matter of pride,' Kemal said in that same quiet voice. 'Can I do less than follow the wishes of a guest in my grandfather's house?'

Delia said nothing—there seemed little she could say in reply to such an enigmatic remark, and Madame Renoir was already pointing out one of the brightly painted horse-drawn carriages that passed by as Kemal turned into a car park. 'The *payton* is the only way to see Antalya properly,' she told Delia. 'They are very *pittoresque*, no?'

'Lovely,' Delia agreed readily, and turned to look at the smart horse-drawn cab, painted bright red and gleaming with burnished brass lamps. 'Can we really go sightseeing in one of those?'

Kemal did not reply, but lent a hand to his aunt as she got out of the car, then turning to offer Delia his help he held her gaze and his mouth smiled faintly as he looked down at her steadily for a moment. 'Since you are set on playing the tourist, *hanim*,' he told her quietly, 'the *payton* is the best way to travel.'

Delia could feel the wild hammering of her heartbeat when his strong brown fingers curled over her bare arm and she hastily avoided the steady gaze of those dark eyes as she stepped out of the car and stood beside him for a moment while he locked the car door. She was so uncertain of his true feelings in the matter of his acting as her guide that she wished for a moment that she and Madame Renoir could have come alone.

'I'm sorry if my being a—a tourist embarrasses you, Mr. Selim,' she told him in a small unsteady voice, 'but you don't have to bother if you'd rather not. I can go alone quite easily—or with Madame Renoir, I don't mind!'

'Ah, but of course we will come with you, *chérie*!' Madame Renoir insisted, and she looked at her nephew with a hint of reproach in her eyes. 'Kemal is not serious about calling you the tourist, he only teases you!'

Delia was quite sure that her own reading of the situation was the more accurate, however, and she looked up at Kemal with a bright gleam of challenge in her green eyes, her heart thudding anxiously at her ribs. 'I don't think so, *madame*,' she said. 'Mr. Selim hasn't a very good opinion of me, I have no illusions on that score, and since he seems to find my wanting to see the sights an embarrassment to him, I'd much rather find my own way around than be any further trouble to him!'

She was being quite unforgivably rude, Delia knew it, but some instinct she could not control seemed to be goading her into letting Kemal know that she was fully aware of how he felt, no matter what veneer of good manners he put on to disguise it.

Madame Renoir looked startled and it was evident that she was unsure what to do or say next, but Kemal's reaction was quicker. He curled his strong fingers once more around Delia's arm, his palm smooth and warm against her soft skin and arousing a sensation not unlike panic in her unsteady emotions as he looked down at her.

'You claim to know me very well, *hanim*,' he told her, his deep voice as steady as a rock, and

Delia instinctively shook her head to deny it.

'I know you don't—I know you didn't want to come at all,' she insisted a little breathlessly. 'And there's really no need for you to act as guide as well now that we're here.'

The fingers on her arm tightened their grip until Delia felt like crying out in protest. 'So you think you can dismiss me like a *hamal* now that I have served your purpose, *hanim*?' he asked in a stern cold voice, and Delia licked her lips anxiously but did not reply. 'Both you and *madame*, my aunt, are under my protection,' Kemal went on relentlessly, 'and whether you wish it or not I shall not allow you to walk the streets alone!'

Delia felt herself trembling, mostly because of the firm hold on her arm and the proximity of his person. There was a stunning aura of maleness about him that seemed to touch every nerve in her body, a fierce masculine arrogance that had her senses reeling, and she could find no words, but simply nodded her head without speaking.

'Kemal!' Madame spoke softly and one gentle hand on his was enough to remind him that they were in a public place. After a moment he let his hand slide from Delia's arm and stood for a moment just looking down at her as if there was more, much more, that he would like to have said.

Then he shrugged his broad shoulders resignedly. '*Iyiyim*,' he murmured, and Madame Renoir made no secret of her relief.

'Shall we go?' she suggested, and Delia too breathed an inward sigh of relief when he nodded.

Crossing swords with Kemal Selim could be much more alarming than she had anticipated, and she would be hesitant about trying it again.

The hooves of the ponies were a pleasant accompaniment to their ride as they clip-clopped on the road through the sunny streets, inducing an air of somnolence with their rhythm, and Delia curled her fingers into moist palms as she coped with a variety of sensations that made her head spin.

Madame Renoir sat on one side of her in the red-painted *payton* as they drove through Antalya, and Kemal sat on the other, and in the limited space available it was impossible to avoid close contact with her companions. It was this proximity in fact that was the sensation Delia found hardest of all to cope with.

A soft fabric hood, rather like a large pram hood, sheltered them from the sun and the soft, musical sound of the cab's warning bell added to the general air of unreality so that in other circumstances Delia might have imagined she was dreaming the whole thing. But the pressure of Kemal's hard thigh against her own was real enough to be infinitely disturbing and she was all too aware of the virile, masculine nearness of him pressed close to her and making it hard for her to control her reactions.

The smoothness of his jacket sleeve brushed her bare arm each time he moved, and there was a spicy smell of aftershave that was exotic enough to lend credence to the suggestion of Eastern male dominance. She shivered involuntarily, then hastily brought herself back to earth and gave her attention to her surroundings. Kemal Selim was disturbing enough without allowing such fancies to invade her thoughts.

The driver of the *payton*, perched up on his box in front of them, seemed to know exactly where they were going, so Delia assumed that the brief conversation in Turkish with Kemal before they started had given him his directions. They rode around the town with both Kemal and Madame Renoir pointing out items of interest.

To Delia, Kemal's participation in her education came as something of a surprise, although his grandfather had promised he would prove an excellent instructor in the wonders of their country. His deep, quiet voice had the effect of making even the most mundane information sound of outstanding interest, and after a while, she noticed, Madame Renoir yielded most of the talking to him and was mainly content to sit back and enjoy the ride.

Most intriguing to Delia were the street vendors with their amazing variety of wares for sale and she found herself trying to discover how many different ones there were. They sold everything from razor blades to brightly coloured balloons, and from cheap sun-glasses to lottery tickets, all offered with the same earnest exaggeration of worth, and none short of buyers.

They rode around for much longer than Delia realised until Madame Renoir suggested lunch was long overdue, and a glance at her wristwatch revealed that it was much later than she realised. The big canvas bag containing her things for the beach was tucked away out of sight in the boot of the car and she never once thought about the promised swim, there was much too much to see in Antalya itself.

They lunched in a restaurant that catered for visitors rather than one of the more national ones, possibly because Kemal was almost as traditionalist as his grandfather was at heart, and a European girl would cause less comment where visitors were customary.

The meal, however, was as Turkish as anything Delia had had at Mavisu and she made no demur when Kemal suggested items from the menu that she would like. She felt strangely content with him somehow and even one or two curious glances from other customers did little to disturb her.

There was no chance of her being mistaken for a Turkish girl with her short red-gold hair and green eyes, and Kemal was so dark that the contrast was perhaps startling to someone noticing them for the first time, but that did not worry her either. It was the first time she had really felt at ease with him and even now there was an exciting flutter of sensation in her pulses each time he looked directly at her.

A light vegetable soup was followed by the traditional *sis kebab*, and Delia was in the process of exploring a delicious concoction of pastry, nuts and syrup when she caught a glimpse of Madame Renoir's sudden change of expression. A plump elegant hand was laid gently on Kemal's arm and she inclined her head very briefly in the direction of the wide open doors.

Kemal frowned, she saw that in the look she gave him from the corners of her eyes, and she was curious enough to glance swiftly but discreetly in the same direction. At first she could see nothing untoward about the several customers arriving and leaving, but then she noticed the young woman alone, and instinctively she knew that she was the reason for Madame Renoir's gently warning hand on Kemal's arm.

Obviously one of the new, rising generation of Turkish women who are gradually emerging from the restrictions of their past, the woman carried herself with an elegant grace that spoke of boundless self-confidence. She was striking-looking, even in a country of darkly striking faces, and when she saw her Delia's heart began to rap hard at her ribs for some inexplicable reason.

The newcomer came across the restaurant, defying the convention that says women do not appear unaccompanied in public places, sweeping between the small tables with an air that defied anyone to remark on her being there. She was about half way across the room when she saw Kemal, and Delia, from the shadow of her lashes, saw her hesitate.

There was no doubt who it was she recognised and a moment later she changed direction and came towards them on long elegant legs, a smile on her face that suggested the air of self-confidence had just taken a blow, and Delia wondered who on earth she was.

Getting to his feet, Kemal inclined his head in that same stiff mockery of a bow that Delia was familiar with and she could not even guess what was going on behind those strong dark features. Whether the woman's arrival had disturbed him or not was impossible to tell, for even that initial frown was missing now.

'*Merhaba*, Kemal.' The dark eyes stayed on Kemal for several seconds before she recognised that he was in company. '*Gün aydın, madame*.' She smiled at the older woman, but the smile disappeared when she looked at Delia and a small frown drew black brows together above curious eyes.

'Suna!' Kemal's voice was coolly polite and obviously much more formal than the newcomer had expected, for a faint flush coloured the smooth high cheekbones as she looked again at Delia. 'Our guest is English,' Kemal explained, 'Miss Delia Crompton! Delia Hanim, may I introduce Suna Kozlu, a very old friend.' He indicated a chair beside his aunt. 'Will you join us?'

Delia was still recovering from the fact that he had at long last used the more informal manner of address and added her christian name, something he had never done before, and she wondered why he had done so now. She glanced at Suna Kozlu's smooth handsome features and tried to guess just what that term 'old friend' had implied.

However close they might have been, Delia decided, there must have been a change of heart somewhere along the line, for Kemal's attitude

44

scarcely suggested anything more close than a casual acquaintance at the moment, and Suna Kozlu was shaking her head in response to the invitation to join them. 'I have little time,' she explained, but Delia suspected that her own presence had quite a lot to do with the refusal, and the glance from those dark eyes was unfriendly to say the least as the woman took her leave.

For several moments nothing was said and Delia felt the tension in the atmosphere as she quietly got on with her *baklava*. Looking up, she caught Madame Renoir's eye and the older woman smiled, a little ruefully, Delia thought. 'Suna Kozlu is one of the new breed of Turkish women,' she said quietly. 'She is to be a doctor next year and will do well, I think.'

Being unaware of whether Suna Kozlu was married or not, Delia ventured a question in that direction, first glancing at Kemal from the corners of her eyes. 'It's unusual to see a Turkish woman so free to go about on her own,' she said. 'Doesn't her husband mind?'

Madame Renoir said nothing but glanced swiftly at Kemal, who raised one dark brow and determinedly held Delia's gaze as he spoke. 'Suna Kozlu is not prepared to sacrifice her profession for marriage,' he said in a cool flat voice. 'She has no husband.'

Knowing she was treading on delicate ground, Delia nevertheless ventured further. 'Couldn't she have both?' she asked, and once again met the deep

45

glowing darkness of Kemal's eyes as he looked at her steadily.

'There may be men prepared to accept her on those terms,' he told her quietly. 'I would not!'

CHAPTER THREE

DELIA sat with a list balanced across her knees, ostensibly recording the latest finds unearthed from the dig, but somehow her mind kept straying from the job in hand to matters much less historic and more persistent. She was seated on a small canvas stool outside the site's tent and her feet were tucked up under her as she gazed pensively across into the thick, lush vegetation that surrounded her. Lost in thought, she absently chewed the tip of her pencil, one elbow resting on her knee.

The exotic surroundings contributed nothing to a subject as mundane as making entries on a list of archaeological finds, and instead the heady scents of magnolias and roses helped to lull her into a trance-like state of being half asleep. She pondered on what it must be like to live permanently in a place like Mavisu and found such luxury hard to imagine as a permanent state of affairs.

The house itself was beautiful, but the grounds were even more exotic, the lush, beautiful gardens that were like something out of a dream to a girl brought up among the neat sameness of an English suburb. It was not the first time Delia had speculated on the idea of staying at Mavisu for the rest of her life, and yet she could never quite see herself as the right type to fit in with such surroundings.

A petite redhead with curly hair and green eyes surely did not belong in such an exotic setting, she thought, and once again the vague image of a smooth, golden-skinned face with dark eyes intruded into her daydreams so that she shook her head impatiently to rid herself of it. Suna Kozlu would fit perfectly into such a background, but Delia disliked the idea of that more than she cared to admit.

The unexpected meeting with Suna Kozlu during her visit to Antalya with Kemal and his aunt had given rise to a great deal of thought on Delia's part, and she wondered just how close the Turkish girl's relationship was, or had been, with Kemal.

It had been obvious, to Delia at least, that Suna Kozlu felt something pretty deep for him, for it had shown quite plainly both in her manner and in those expressive dark eyes when she first saw him. But it was Kemal's feelings that puzzled Delia, for they were much less evident, and she had pondered the question ever since.

A little impatient at her own preoccupation with Kemal's affairs, she brought herself back to reality once more and glanced over her shoulder at Clifford and her uncle working on the site. She made a wry grimace of regret for her lack of interest of late and told herself that she really ought to show a more active concern for what they were doing.

According to Professor Crompton's theory, and it seemed more than likely that he was right in the light of recent events, this corner of Sadi Selim's gardens had once housed a temple to Artemis, the ancient Greek goddess of the hunt, and it was not at all difficult to imagine a goddess being worshipped in such surroundings. The setting was so right, and the idea of men worshipping a goddess appealed to her feminine vanity in her present mood.

Again she glanced over her shoulder and once more felt that irresistible restlessness, impatient because she was unsure of the reason for it. Her uncle was busy, his whole attention on what he was doing, and Delia had no doubt that he would have found her romantic vision of history amusing. He might be interested in the goddess to the exclusion of everything else at the moment, but his interest was strictly practical and left no room for the kind of romanticism that Delia had in mind.

Dragging herself back to earth yet again, she was aware that she was being watched and she looked across at Clifford toiling away beside her uncle. He straightened his back as she looked at him briefly, one hand brushing the moisture from his forehead while his grey eyes held hers steadily, curious and speculative behind their dark-rimmed spectacles.

Ever since her visit to Antalya Clifford's attitude had both puzzled her and made her uneasy, for he seemed always to be watching her in that same tense, curious way he did now. He had said little about her outing, except to ask if she had enjoyed herself, but she felt that he still resented her going with Kemal instead of asking him to take her.

Gazing down at the list on her knees, she absently drew a question mark in one corner and tried to decide whether it mattered to her what Clifford felt. 'Delia!' She started and looked up hastily when he spoke from right beside her, then a moment later laughed at her own nervousness.

'You startled me!' she told him. 'I didn't hear you!'

Clifford's grey eyes had a dark, unhappy look that caused her a momentary twinge of conscience, although she could not imagine why it should. He squatted down beside her, supporting himself with one hand on a section of broken column they had unearthed the day before, and looked at her for several seconds before he spoke again.

'You seemed to be far away,' he said, and watched her closely as he spoke. 'Are you restless again, Delia?'

Uncertain just what her mood was, Delia affected interest in her list for a few moments. 'I don't think I'm restless,' she denied, but even while she was denying it she was forced to recognise that he was right. 'You must be imagining things, Clifford!'

'I don't think so!' He spoke with more authority than Delia would have expected of him and she frowned briefly at his tone.

'I'm perfectly happy,' she insisted quietly. 'I can't think what gives you the idea I'm not.'

'Because I know you!'

His hand under her chin was unexpectedly firm and he turned her face towards him so that she could see the frown that drew his brows together and the tightness at the corners of his mouth. She thought for a moment that he was going to kiss her, for the promise of it was there in his eyes, and her instinct was to turn away her head, but then he released her and his fingers slid from her chin as he shook his head slowly—resignedly.

'You *don't* know me, Clifford,' she told him in the same quiet voice, despite a trembling sense of indecision that made her unsure of anything. Then she half-smiled, trying to restore normality. 'And I *am* quite happy, no matter what you think!'

Clifford said nothing for a moment, but he straightened up suddenly and shrugged his shoulders, one hand brushing back the hair from his forehead. 'It's something in your manner,' he told her after a while. 'You seem—I don't know, restless and as if you're——' He looked down at her with a hint of challenge in his grey eyes. 'You're not thinking of going off on another trip with Selim, are you, Delia?' he asked.

The question sounded so much like an accusation that she instinctively resented it and she got to her feet, her eyes searching his face for some sign of the old familiar Clifford. There had been a change lately and she was not at all sure that she liked it. His newly acquired aggressiveness could be taken for a form of flattery, she supposed, but it made her uneasy and even more uncertain of her own feelings.

'I haven't been invited out again,' she told him, 'but if I am I shall go! I enjoyed myself and I see no reason to deny it!'

'Because you went with Selim!' Clifford accused, and Delia shook her head impatiently.

'Madame Renoir's being there makes nonsense of what you're suggesting,' she told him frankly, and noticed that he was making less effort to keep his voice down now.

'I'm not suggesting anything,' Clifford denied, a bright angry gleam in his eyes. 'I just don't want you to get too involved with Selim, that's all, because I'd hate you to get hurt, Delia, and you will, believe me, you will!'

'I'm not a complete idiot!' Delia declared angrily, a bright flush in her cheeks. 'And you're very wide of the mark, Clifford, if you think Kemal has anything like that in mind!'

'Kemal?' He echoed her use of Kemal's first name in a voice harsh with anger, and she curled her hands tightly as she tried to control her churning emotions.

'I refuse to argue with you!' she said in a small tight voice, and put down the half completed list on the stool behind her. 'I'm going,' she told him, and smoothed anxious hands down the brief shorts she wore with a short sleeved shirt and sandals.

'Delia?' Clifford frowned at her worriedly, sparing a brief look in the direction of her uncle. 'Where are you going?'

'It doesn't matter where I'm going,' Delia told him, her chin held at a defiant angle. 'Kemal Selim isn't coming with me—that's all that need concern you!'

It was possibly an unkind remark to make, but her own feelings were too involved to allow her to act reasonably and she parted the mass of scented foliage in front of her, letting it close to behind her again, heedless of Clifford's anxious voice as she walked away.

'Delia, please!' She knew he would be casting anxious glances at her uncle, wondering if he dared follow instead of going back to his work, and she felt a momentary twinge of conscience, but refused to turn around and go back to him. 'Delia!'

Her head held high, Delia walked on through the dense growth of scented shrubs and trees, the waxy blossoms of magnolias brushing coolly against her flushed cheeks as she went. She had nothing on her head, for she had been in shade while she sat on the stool, and the first thing that struck her was the intense heat of the sun as she walked out on to the driveway.

It was possibly foolhardy to venture any farther dressed as she was, but her mood was not reasonable at the moment and she felt a strange mixture of anger and excitement as she walked down the driveway, not towards the house but to the gates that gave access to the hot dusty road outside.

The mingled scents and the soft sighing wind that blew off the sea below the cliffs lent a deceptive coolness to the air and all combined to add to her mood so that she was unconcerned at the moment where she went. The tall iron gates were fastened but not locked, and she opened them and stepped outside almost without realising she was doing it.

All along by the wall that bordered the gardens the shade of overhanging plane trees made it blessedly cool, and Delia put back her head to let the warm breeze blow over her face and the flushed pinkness of her cheeks, her eyes half closed. At home, going for a walk to cool off in the circumstances would have been the natural thing to do, and she saw nothing wrong with doing so now because she did not even stop to think about it.

She presented an incongruous figure walking along the hot dusty road, her slim legs bare and tanned to a pale gold below brief blue cotton shorts, and a thin cotton shirt emphasising the slender curves above them. Cars came this way, but they were infrequent and the only foot travellers were likely to be the local village people with their donkeys or horses, the womenfolk clad from head to toe and for the most part discreetly veiled from strange male eyes.

Her own brief apparel would cause considerable consternation should she meet anyone, but at the moment it did not occur to her. Nothing mattered except the prospect of a change of scene. Below her, at the end of the mountain road, Antalya sat like a jewel in the sun, its small bay and turquoise blue waters shimmering like silk shot with gold.

It looked so close from where she was and she had never before realised that the town might be within walking distance, so that for a second she toyed with the idea of walking all the way down there.

The road gave a view of the sea that was indescribably beautiful, soaring high above it with a mass of lush vegetation growing right to the very edge and a cool stream some yards ahead rushing down from the mountains, ice cold and glittering like silver in the sun to cascade over the edge of the coral-coloured rocks into the sea.

It was breathtaking and not quite real, like most of this beautiful coast, and it worked wonders with Delia's restless spirit, but she suddenly found herself wishing she could see more of such scenes, of towns like Antalya—and Kemal Selim would make an ideal guide.

Impatiently she shrugged off the persistent image of Kemal, because always when she thought of him she recalled the tall elegance of Suna Kozlu, the Turkish girl who wanted to be a doctor even if it meant her staying single. Suna Kozlu intrigued her simply because she could not decide whether or not Kemal returned her obvious affection for him.

A wide shady plane tree spanned half the roadway at one point and offered some relief from the heat of the sun. It also offered a breathtaking view from its far side if she stood in its shade right at the edge of the cliff, and Delia paused for a moment to make the most of both its advantages. Leaning back against the tree, she curled her arms backwards around it and looked down at the sea, although her mind was not entirely on the scenery.

Yet again Kemal Selim invaded her thoughts and just as determinedly Delia tried to dismiss him. Clifford was right, of course; she could get hurt very easily by a man like Kemal, and if she did it would be difficult to blame anyone but herself, for she had so far received not the slightest encouragement. If Kemal found her attractive at all, which he showed no sign of doing, it would merely be as a passing fancy, a brief amusement—Clifford was a much safer proposition.

Delia was so caught up in her own rather discomfiting musings that it was a moment or two before she realised there was a car coming up the hill from Antalya. She had seen no one until now and it occurred to her suddenly that anyone seeing her there beside the road dressed as she was could be forgiven for coming to quite the wrong conclusions.

Instinctively she moved round the huge trunk of the tree and as far out of sight as she could from anyone on the road. It was not certain, of course, that a passing motorist would be curious enough to stop, but supposing they did she had no way of knowing what opportunities a man might see in such an encounter.

A smooth gear change coped with the increasing incline and a second later the sound of the engine grew louder when the car came round the bend in the road. Thinking herself out of sight, Delia listened, waiting for the car to pass and the sound to fade away, but instead the engine was cut suddenly and the car stopped, only yards from where she stood.

A door slammed and the heavy tread of male feet approached from the other side of the tree while Delia stood there, her eyes briefly closed in a prayer for the ability to cope with the offer of an unwanted lift, and possibly a driver misled by appearances as well. Without turning her head she could sense the scrutiny of curious eyes and the first inkling of realisation dawned as she turned at last and looked into the dark, frowning face of Kemal Selim.

Her heart lurched crazily when the brown eyes met hers head on and she almost smiled her relief, only his expression discouraged any such levity. There was a stern disapproving look in the eyes that noticed her bright, red-gold head was without a hat, and her fingers curled, scraping against the bark of the tree as she licked her lips anxiously, avoiding his gaze.

He missed nothing—the slender bare legs and the brevity of the blue cotton shorts, the thin shirt that was stretched across the young curves of her body where her arms pulled it tight, and the flimsy sandals that made poor walking on the hot, stony road.

'Are you quite mad, *çocuk*?' Kemal asked sternly, and Delia shook her head, too stunned for the moment to object to his question or the tone of his voice. 'Why are you out here?' he demanded. 'And in that—that costume? Have you no sense?'

Delia glanced down at her bare legs and suddenly felt as if she had appeared in public stark naked and quite brazen about it. Her shirt too, clinging to her figure, felt much too thin and flimsy for decency, and she moved her arms from around the trunk of the tree and folded them across her breast in a curiously defensive gesture. Why, she thought desperately, did he have to make her feel as if she should be ashamed?

'I—I only came out for a walk,' she said after a moment, and Kemal swept his dark gaze over her swiftly.

'Like that?' he asked.

Defensiveness was giving way to resentment gradually and Delia thrust out her chin in a gesture that was meant to deny his right to criticise her or the way she dressed. 'I didn't stop to change,' she told him, 'but you don't have to look at me as if——'

'I am looking at you as any other man would!' Kemal Selim interrupted coldly, a coldness that was belied by the dark glitter in his eyes. 'What would you have done if a stranger had stopped and taken your—invitation at its face value?'

'Invitation?' Delia stared at him indignantly, scarcely believing he meant it seriously. 'You surely can't believe I came out here to——' She curled her hands tightly over her bare arms and she was trembling like a leaf as she looked at him. 'How *dare* you!' she whispered huskily, but Kemal merely looked at her down the length of his haughty nose.

Her slim bare legs felt so much more conspicuous suddenly and she would have given much to walk off and leave him, but her legs felt quite incredibly shaky and unsteady. Also she would have to brush past him to get to the road and at the moment she had not the nerve to do it.

Kemal regarded her steadily. 'Do you imagine

that Turks are different from other men?' he asked, and Delia shook her head. She should be angry, but her heart was pulsating so violently and there was a curious trickle of warning tingling through her body as she looked at him.

'No; no, of course not,' she said in a small tight voice.

The dark eyes held hers steadily despite her frantic longing to look away. 'A natural modesty protects our womenfolk, *hanim*,' he said in a soft quiet voice, 'but offered such a display of soft pale skin so freely displayed, why should a man not feel himself entitled to take what he sees?'

The huge trunk of the tree was firmly set at her back and she wondered dizzily if his warning applied only to others of his countrymen or if it voiced his own reactions too—if it did there was no way of escape for her. She looked at him for a moment, trembling and uncertain, but strengthened by a certain defiance too, her green eyes wide and wary.

'You—you talk as if I was some—some immoral little——'

'I suggested nothing of the sort,' Kemal denied firmly but quietly. 'But you were surely not intending to walk into Antalya looking as you do, were you, *hanim*?'

'Why not?' Delia could not resist the retort, although she had never seriously intended to walk so far or to appear in the town dressed as she was.

There was a tenseness about him, she realised suddenly, a taut straightness about his mouth that sent little shivers of warning along her spine as she looked at him, but far from feeling alarmed Delia felt suddenly and quite unbelievably lightheaded.

Kemal's dark eyes swept over her again, but not swiftly and angrily this time. Now the gaze was slow and explicit, taking in every curve of her slender shape so that she shivered and hugged her arms still more closely to her body.

'Why not?' He echoed her question, his voice warm and deep and so blatantly sensual that it played havoc with her senses. 'Are you such a child, Delia, that you have to ask me that?'

His use of her christian name and the bright glowing darkness of his eyes were both unexpected and infinitely disturbing, and she shook her head slowly, like someone in a dream. Above all was the effect of that deep, sensuous voice that stirred unfamiliar longings in her and her heart was beating so wildly that she felt breathless as she tried hard to control it.

'I—I'm not a child at all,' she denied in a small husky voice. 'And no matter what you think, Kemal Bey, I wasn't trying to attract attention to myself. I —I disagreed with Clifford—Mr. Aitkin—and I simply walked off and left him. Anyway,' she added trying to re-establish her right to be dressed as she pleased, 'it didn't really matter how I was dressed, because I haven't seen anyone!'

Kemal held her reluctant gaze for a second or two and just for a moment a brief smile touched his mouth, softening its stern outline. Then he reached out with his hands suddenly, and firmly but gently pulled her arms apart, holding her for a moment with her hands in his, spread wide while he looked down the slim length of her body. The warmth of his nearness enveloped her, spiced with a masculine scent that recalled for her the last time she had been this close to him.

'You saw me,' Kemal said quietly. 'Do you think me any less impressionable than any other man?' Again the dark eyes swept over her, making her conscious of the brevity of her costume and the hard strong hands that held her arms apart. 'You should learn that to offer your body so freely for men to see is not always wise, *küçük*, and perhaps I am the one to teach you, hmm?'

Delia was too dazed to try and evade him and in her heart she was not even sure that she wanted to. She shivered as he drew her closer and instinctively put out her hands to the broad firm chest, her open palms warmed by the golden skin through his thin shirt.

He bent his head and his mouth touched the soft-ness of her throat, a light, breathless touch that sent her senses whirling out of control as she closed her eyes. With a slow deliberation that was exciting in itself his mouth moved to a spot at the side of her neck, strong fingers curling slowly into the soft red-gold hair and pulling it aside, caressing her warm skin as they did so.

Strong gentle hands slid the cotton shirt down from her shoulders and he kissed the smoothness of her neck and shoulders, his mouth firm and sen-suous and arousing such sensations in her that Delia almost cried out. Nothing she had ever imagined

60

had been like this and she must wake at any moment and find it was all a dream.

There was nothing dreamlike about the taut, hard body that held her close, demanding so much, nor the hands that brought shivers of sensation with their gentle, firm persuasion, but she could not really believe it was happening. The wild uncontrollable excitement that seared through her body made her yield to the sudden fierce pressure of his mouth on hers and there was nothing she could do to fight the needs of her own body.

It was as if someone had suddenly taken the warmth from the sun when Kemal released her only seconds later, and Delia stood for a second, her mind in chaos, her brain spinning with the unexpectedness of it. Kemal stood with his back to her, his dark head bent against the arm that stretched out straight in front of him, the hand flat palmed against the trunk of the plane tree.

'That should not have happened, Delia Hanim,' he said in the firm cool voice she was more accustomed to, and for a second Delia stared at the broad back presented to her with wide unbelieving eyes.

Her hands, her whole body, trembled with the emotional shock of the last few minutes and she could not yet face the fact of his apparent calmness. 'Please,' she whispered after several seconds. 'Don't —don't apologise.'

He turned suddenly and looked down at her, and his dark eyes blazed with some inner passion that even now made her tremble at the sight of it. 'You are a guest in my grandfather's house,' he said, still unbelievably cool and matter-of-fact. 'It was ill-mannered to take such advantage of a lady under his protection.'

Delia stared at him in dismay, her eyes stunned into blankness and as green as the leaves of the plane tree with the sun shining through them. It was not easy to forget the hard urgency of his body while he had held her, and she could still feel the impression of his strong hands tingling on her skin, and yet he was quite composedly passing off those few wildly exciting moments as merely a breach of good manners.

'Ill—ill-mannered?' She swallowed hard and shook her head slowly, like someone in a dream. 'Is that all——'

Kemal frowned and it was obvious that he found her reaction not only unexpected but dis-comfitingly naïve. Delia turned away swiftly, unable to face him now that he realised how deeply that brief episode had affected her, and tried to recover some of her composure.

She heard him move, but he did not touch her, merely came and stood close behind her so that she was still aware of the enveloping warmth of him and curled her hands tightly. 'Come,' he said quietly, 'I will take you back!'

He turned and walked back towards the car, but Delia did not follow him as he obviously expected her to and when he realised it he turned and looked back at her. She still stood there under the huge plane tree, small and somehow very vulnerable, and she shook her head when he raised an enquiring brow.

'I'll walk back, thank you,' she said, and her voice sounded so small that it barely carried the few short yards to where he stood watching her, the car door open, ready for her.

For a moment she thought he would simply get into the car and drive away, leaving her there, and she felt she would have hated him for it if he had, but instead he came back towards her and she felt her heart thudding wildly as she put her arms once more around the plane tree as if clinging to it would prevent his taking her back by force.

His expressive dark eyes were half hidden by the short thick lashes that surrounded them and he looked down at her for several seconds before he spoke. 'You will come back with me, *hanim*,' he insisted quietly. 'I have already broken the code of hospitality once because of you, you will not force me to do so again!'

One large hand was extended towards her and, uncertain whether she was meant to take it or simply treat it as an indication of direction, Delia hesitated briefly, then walked past him towards the car on legs that trembled as if they would at any moment collapse under her.

Kemal saw her into the car in silence, then walked round and got in beside her. He turned in his seat to look at her, then shook his head slowly, and she wondered if it really was a hint of smile she saw twitching the corner of his wide mouth. 'I assume that you will be complaining to your uncle about my behaviour,' he said, as if there was absolutely no doubt in his mind, but Delia shook her head.

The idea of telling Uncle Arthur about Kemal having kissed her would mean little to him. He knew Sadi Selim and he looked upon both the old man and his grandson as men after his own heart, he would see nothing wrong in the younger one kissing his niece—only Clifford would feel outraged at the idea, and she certainly did not propose telling Clifford!

'I shan't tell anyone,' she denied huskily, and carefully avoided looking at him as she said it.

Kemal studied her for a second through narrowed eyes, then he shrugged. 'Your native penchant for freedom!' he remarked dryly. 'You consider it of no concern to the professor that you are at such risk walking about alone? That such things can happen to you that you have no control over?'

Delia found the temptation too much to resist, and she felt it worth risking his anger to be revenged for that coldly formal ending to their embrace. Her chin was high and her green eyes glistened with satisfaction as she turned and looked at him. 'Oh, but according to you, Kemal Bey,' she said in a deceptively meek voice, 'it wouldn't have happened at all if I hadn't been walking about practically naked—Uncle Arthur wouldn't blame you, how could he? And Clifford already thinks you have designs on me, so he wouldn't be surprised either!'

The expression Kemal used was short, terse and, unless Delia was very much mistaken, extremely virulent, and his eyes blazed as he looked down at her. 'You treat such matters very lightly, *hanim*!' he told her in a cold hard voice. 'But be assured that Mr. Aitkin need have no worry about your future safety in my hands—you are more of a child than I had realised!'

He turned away abruptly and started the engine, and the muscles of his thigh where it pressed against her warned Delia that he was angrier than she had expected, and somehow, despite that angry jibe about her youth, it gave her a curious satisfaction to realise it.

CHAPTER FOUR

MADAME RENOIR was looking at Delia enquiringly and there was a hint of that familiar mischief in her light brown eyes as she leaned towards her across the corner of the table. 'You are daydreaming, *petite*, huh?' she asked, and laughed delightedly when Delia blinked herself hastily back to reality.

'I suppose I was,' Delia admitted with a smile. 'I'm sorry, *madame*.'

'*Mais non*, why should you be sorry?' Madame Renoir demanded good-naturedly. 'Young girls are entitled to dream, especially about *l'amour*, eh, *chérie*?'

65

It was purely an instinctive movement when Delia glanced at Kemal before she replied and she did not even realise she had done so until he met and held her gaze. 'Oh no, *madame*!' she denied hastily, avoiding those faintly curious eyes. 'I—I wasn't thinking about anything in particular, just, as you say, daydreaming. There's nothing I can do on the site this afternoon, so I shall probably go in search of one of those lovely cold streams that come down from the mountains.'

'You mean to walk?' Madame Renoir asked, quite obviously thinking the idea quite mad. 'But in this heat, *chérie*, you will be exhausted!'

Delia smiled and shook her head. It was an idea she had entertained for some time now and she had no intention of allowing Madame Renoir's well-meaning concern to put her off. 'I was thinking of going up into the forest, the woods just off the road,' she explained. 'It won't be hot among the trees, but I'll wear a hat anyway.' She laughed softly, already revelling in the idea of cool running water. 'The thought of that icy cold water is irresistible!'

Madame Renoir still looked dubious, however, and the glances she cast in Kemal's direction suggested that she expected him to intervene, to try and dissuade Delia from going, but Kemal was, to all appearances, oblivious of either the proposed venture or the need for his intervention. Clifford on the other hand had caught the general gist of the plan and it was obvious that he was unhappy about it.

He frowned across at Delia anxiously, a morsel of

pilâv suspended on his fork, half way to his mouth. 'Are you planning to go somewhere this afternoon, Delia?' he asked, and the slightly defiant angle of her chin when she looked at him was echoed by the look in her eyes.

'I'm just going for a short walk on my own,' Delia told him. 'Only a few yards along the road and up into the trees, so there's absolutely nothing for you to look so concerned about, Clifford.'

Clifford's grey eyes gleamed determinedly behind his glasses and he leaned across the table towards her, his voice low but none the less firm. 'I'll come with you,' he declared. 'You're not traipsing around in the woods on your own, Delia, heaven knows what you'll come across!'

Delia frowned at him impatiently. 'Oh, Clifford, for heaven's sake! I shan't meet anything more dangerous than a—a mountain goat—there isn't anything more dangerous than that so near to a town, I'm sure of it! I don't *need* you to come with me, or anyone else, I'll be perfectly all right on my own!'

'You don't know that you won't meet anything,' Clifford argued firmly. 'There *are* other things than goats on the slopes of the hills, Delia, and I don't like you going up there alone!'

Neither of them had raised their voices above a normal quiet conversational tone, but Kemal was looking at her suddenly and she knew without doubt that he had overheard, and also that he would find the temptation to intervene too much to resist. She studiously avoided looking at him, but for all that her cheeks warmed with colour under his scrutiny and she hated herself for being so susceptible.

'If you mean to go into the woods, *hanim*, you would be wise to have someone with you,' he said quietly, and flicked a brief glance at Clifford seated beside him. 'I regret that I cannot offer my services in this instance because I have an appointment elsewhere, but you would be better advised not to go alone—these woods are not as much like your English woodland as you might suppose.'

'There's no need for her to go alone,' Clifford told him shortly. 'I've already said I'll go with her!'

Professor Crompton and Sadi Selim had momentarily abandoned their own discussion and were now taking an interest in what was being said, possibly attracted by the edge of sharpness on Clifford's voice and his unmistakable tension. Thanks to Delia's intervention Clifford had taken two days off from the dig recently and driven with her to Perge and Aspendos to see the ancient city ruins and the theatre, but the professor was likely to look askance at yet another request for absence.

He frowned discouragingly at Clifford, his short-sighted eyes peering at him through their lenses. 'I hope you're not making any rash promises, my boy,' the professor told him, and Clifford shrugged, almost as if he was already resigned to seeing his plans quashed, and in the circumstances Delia could not help feeling sorry for him.

'Delia can't go alone, Professor,' he insisted. 'We don't really know what's in those woods.'

'I suppose there is some element of risk involved,' the professor allowed, and looked at his host enquiringly. 'Your mountain forests aren't quite like our innocent landscape, eh, my friend?' he asked, and Sadi Selim nodded agreement.

'One can never be certain,' he said, but his dark eyes smiled kindly at Delia, as if to let her know that he joined in the general plan to discourage her only for her own good.

Nodding as if he considered the matter closed, her uncle peered at her closely, shaking his head. 'Then I think you'd better forget the idea for the moment, my dear,' he told her. 'Wait until I can spare Clifford again and then go, hmm?'

Unwilling to abandon her planned outing, Delia merely shrugged, but her disappointment was obvious and Clifford still frowned at her doubtfully. The professor, never one to dwell on a subject other than his own for very long, had already forgotten the matter and returned to his earlier discussion with his host, but Clifford leaned towards her once more and tried to catch her eye.

'Delia,' he said, glancing fleetingly at the professor as he spoke, 'please don't do anything silly, will you?'

'I wasn't intending to do anything silly,' Delia retorted crossly, 'only go a few yards along the road, that's all!'

'But you won't go now?' Clifford insisted, and Delia did not answer.

Madame Renoir, her brown eyes warm with understanding, pressed a plump consoling hand

69

over hers and smiled. 'It is well to wait for Monsieur Aitkin to go with you, *chérie*,' she told her gently. 'Or someone else—as long as you do not take chances, huh?'

'I suppose so,' Delia sighed reluctantly. It was the only drawback to Turkey, she thought, this reluctance to allow equal freedom of movement to men and women, and Clifford seemed as determined to follow it as Kemal or any other of his countrymen.

The *tavuklu pilâv* was a delicious concoction of chicken and rice, and Delia did justice to it, but she was conscious all the time she was eating that Clifford was not the only one watching her. Sure enough, as soon as the meal was over the men went their various ways and Madame Renoir followed her into the *salon*, her brown eyes bright with friendly curiosity.

She took a seat in one of the deep comfortable armchairs near the window, but Delia chose to curl herself up on one of the huge colourful cushions that still scattered the floor of the salon, despite its partial Westernization. It was comparatively cool here with a soft wind blowing across the scents of the gardens from the sea, and Delia decided it was quite her favourite room in this huge, exotic house.

'Delia, *ma chère*!' Madame Renoir smiled, and reached out to touch her head gently with one hand. Delia fully expected a discourse on the excellence of the advice she had been given, but she knew Madame Renoir understood how she felt, much better than anyone else did. 'You are thinking of disobeying your uncle,' the Frenchwoman

70

guessed, and smilingly shook her head. 'He means only to act in your interest, *ma chère*, you should believe that.'

'Oh, I do, of course,' Delia agreed, and smiled ruefully. 'But it doesn't make it any easier to accept, *madame*, I'm just not used to being so—so looked after all the time.'

'And you do not like to be looked after?' Madame Renoir's smile looked as if she doubted the truth of that, and she shook her head slowly. 'You should appreciate being treasured, *petite*, it is not every woman's privilege to be so.'

'I know, *madame*.' Delia looked up and smiled. 'And I do appreciate it, it's just that——'

'You do not like to have your freedom curtailed, hmm?' The older woman smiled understanding. 'But you cannot—how do you say?—have your cake and also eat it, yes?' She laughed softly and shook her head. 'It is not possible, *petite*, even for such a pretty child as you are.'

'I suppose not,' Delia agreed reluctantly, and gazed out of the open windows pensively, her hands clasped round her knees. 'I just wish the thought of those icy cold streams wasn't so tempting, that's all!' She had been so preoccupied with her own disappointment that she had not heard anyone else come into the room and did not realise they were no longer alone until Madame Renoir spoke.

'Ah, Kemal, *mon cher*, you are leaving?'

Delia turned quickly, startled by the unexpected, and she met Kemal's dark, reflective gaze warily. He seemed quite incredibly tall standing almost on top of her as he was, and something in her responded instinctively to that stunning aura of uncompromising masculinity, the fierce proud look in his eyes. Despite the civilising effect of a cream suit that fitted his lean figure as only an expensive tailor could have made it, and a brown shirt and silk tie, there was something savagely feudal about him that suggested a much earlier age and a less civilised one.

'So you have decided to be sensible about your outing to the forest, Delia Hanim?' he said quietly, and the lesser formality of her name set her heart fluttering anxiously as she looked up at him.

She had already decided in her own mind to bow to popular opinion and wait until Clifford was available to take her, but somehow Kemal's rather paternal approval aroused the spirit of rebellion again, and she shrugged carelessly. 'Oh, I shall probably go for a walk presently,' she told him, and tried hard to steady her voice.

Kemal's dark eyes held hers steadily until she could no longer bear the scrutiny and hastily lowered her lashes. 'Even though your uncle has forbidden you to go?' he asked.

'Not forbidden, Kemal Bey,' Delia argued, 'only advised.'

He dismissed any difference with a large hand and frowned down at her. 'But you would defy him?' he insisted.

'It isn't a case of defying anyone,' Delia said. 'I don't have to account to anyone for my movements, Kemal Bey, I'm quite capable of looking after myself, you know—I'm not a child!'

'You tried to tell me so once before,' Kemal reminded her quietly, 'but if you remember, *hanim*, I was not convinced!'

His meaning was unmistakable and his dark eyes glittered at her swift intake of breath and the bright warm colour in her cheeks. It was unforgivable of him to have reminded her of her own inexperience and the way she had been stunned into weakness by his kisses, and her hands trembled as she clasped them together in front of her.

She was aware that Madame Renoir was watching her closely, obviously intrigued by Kemal's reference, although she could not possibly have known anything about their meeting on the hill road. Something in her manner suggested that she guessed there was some episode she did not know about but whose existence intrigued her, and her dark eyes speculated on possibilities.

'You were angry,' Delia said, very quietly and with a hint of defiance in her eyes as she looked at Kemal. 'I wasn't quite sure why, Kemal Bey, and I'm still not.' Her eyes widened and although her heart was hammering uncontrollably at her side she held his gaze determinedly for a long moment. 'Perhaps you're right about me, after all,' she suggested softly. 'I'm too much of a child to understand!'

Kemal lifted his chin, his head held arrogantly high, and looked at her down the length of his autocratic nose for several moments with eyes that glittered as black as jet instead of their customary deep brown, and Delia shivered involuntarily. Then he turned to his aunt and inclined his head in that slight formal bow that Delia now recognised as a sign of his displeasure.

'*Au revoir*, Tante Yvette,' he said in a flat, tight voice, and turned and strode back across the room without saying another word to Delia and closing the door behind him with such infinite care that his very control suggested violence.

'*Mon Dieu!*' Madame Renoir breathed as soon as his footsteps had died away outside. 'What has happened, *enfant*? Why is my Kemal so—so passionate, huh?' She was looking at Delia in such a way that it was obvious nothing short of a full explanation would satisfy her. One soft plump hand rested on Delia's head and she shook her head slowly. 'You can tell me, Delia, yes?'

Delia was reluctant and Madame Renoir recognised it, but it did not lessen her determination. The gentle brown eyes had an unfamiliar resoluteness and she sat upright in her armchair waiting while Delia sought for words. 'It's all rather a storm in a teacup, *madame*,' she told her, and hurried on to explain when her listener looked puzzled. 'It's a lot of fuss about nothing very much.'

'Kemal seems not to agree with you, *mon enfant*,' Madame Renoir told her quietly, and Delia shook her head.

'It started because I argued with Clifford the other day and walked off and left him,' she explained, looking down at her own entwined fingers on her lap. 'I—well, I was rather silly, I suppose. I

74

walked down the hill outside instead of coming back to the house, almost without realising what I was doing, and I was standing a little way down the hill when——' She glanced up swiftly and caught the bright gleam of understanding in Madame Renoir's eyes.

'You came back with Kemal, of course,' she said. 'Ah, now I remember!' Her head shook slowly as she gazed at Delia, and she half smiled. 'It was then, *ma petite*, yes?'

'It was then,' Delia admitted with a sigh. 'Kemal took exception to the way I was dressed, he seemed to think I had gone out in shorts with the specific intention of seducing his countrymen! He—he seemed to think—he said I should learn what could happen if I insisted on going about Turkey half dressed, and——' She was finding it much more difficult now that she came to the part she would rather not have talked about, and Madame Renoir seemed to understand how she felt.

She was shaking her head and smiling, that hint of mischief sparkling in her eyes again. 'I can imagine that Kemal cast himself in the role of your *instructeur*, hmm?' she suggested, and Delia nodded but did not say anything. 'Then why such anger, *enfant*?' Madame Renoir asked gently, then almost immediately answered the question herself. 'No, no,' she said, 'I can imagine why, Delia! He is ashamed to have behaved so with a guest of his grandfather's house, no? And to have done so without the lady's consent—*mon Dieu*! He is angry with himself, not with you, *ma chère*!'

'Not entirely,' Delia denied. 'He—he made some remark about my not telling Uncle Arthur about it, about me taking it all very lightly and—and not caring, and I couldn't resist being sarcastic.' She sat for a second with her hands held in front of her looking down at the fingers she was clasping and unclasping with restless repetition. 'I think Kemal Bey is convinced I'm not only promiscuous,' she said in a small slightly unsteady voice, 'but too young to realise I am.'

'Oh, what nonsense!' Madame Renoir declared firmly, and reached out to cover Delia's restless hands with one of her own. 'Kemal is man enough to realise you are not a child, but he finds the realisation too——' She shrugged her plump shoulders, searching for the right word. 'Give him time, *ma chère*,' she said softly, and with such meaning that Delia looked up swiftly, her eyes big and round with astonishment.

'Oh, but, *madame*,' she said breathlessly, 'there's absolutely no reason for you to suppose—I mean, you have no cause to think that——' She waved her hands helplessly and remembered Clifford's certainty that Madame Renoir had her own reasons for organising that trip to Antalya with Kemal. Hastily she got to her feet, smoothing down her dress with hands that were far from steady. 'I hope you haven't gained the wrong impression, *madame*,' she said without looking at the older woman. 'If Kemal Bay has given you the impression that——'

'Kemal has said nothing,' Madame Renoir assured her quietly, 'and be assured he will not, *ma*

76

chère.' The gentle brown eyes only hinted at curiosity and she smiled. 'But if there is something that you wish to tell me, Delia, I am what you call a good listener, hmm?'

'Oh no, there's nothing!' Delia declared hastily. She stood beside Madame Renoir for several seconds, smoothing her hands down her dress and brushing back the hair from her forehead, aware that those gentle, inquisitive brown eyes were watching her as she coped with the fluttering beat of her heart. Those few moments beside the hill road had meant little or nothing to Kemal and Delia wished she could dismiss them as easily, but she found it impossible. 'I—I think I'll go out for a while,' she said, and Madame Renoir extended an anxious hand.

'Delia!' She would have stayed her, but Delia wanted to get away somewhere on her own and try to bring some kind of order to her chaotic thoughts.

She shook her head slowly, smiling reassurance in case the older woman should think herself responsible for her sudden departure. 'I'll be perfectly safe, *madame*,' she said. 'I'm not going very far and I shall be in the shade for most of the way once I leave the road.' She glanced down at her bright lime green shirt-dress and smiled. It was made of thin cool cotton, but it buttoned fairly high in front and reached to her knees although it was sleeveless. 'I don't think even Kemal can call this dress seductive,' she added, and laughed a little unsteadily. '*Au revoir, madame!*'

Delia walked only a short distance along the road from Mavisu before turning off into the thick clustering trees that came down the steep hillside right to the edge of the road. It was cooler among the trees, as she had guessed it would be, but there were any number of little grassy hillocks and outcrops of rock that made it essential to watch every step.

Here everything was as lush and prolific as it was in the gardens at Mavisu, and Delia knew she had been right to come. Occasionally there were odd sounds among the thickness of the vegetation that gave her a few seconds' misgiving, but she determinedly dismissed all thoughts of anything dangerous and went on.

Climbing the steep incline made her breathless after a while, but she found the exercise remarkably exhilarating and the effort was well worth while, for occasionally among the thick muster of trees she came across small grassy dells that were bright with wild flowers and soft green ferns. It was not long either before she came across not one but several mountain streams, splashing and gurgling their way down the hillside among the rocks and trees.

It was blessedly cool and she even toyed with the idea of taking off her shoes and walking in the water for a while, but the pebbly beds of the streams looked as if they would be uncomfortable walking, so she changed her mind. She did, however, take off her shoes and sit for a while with them in her lap while she dabbled her toes in the running coolness, smiling with pleasure at the sensation.

Something, some sound, indistinct as all the sounds were in the forest, made her start and she looked across to where she thought it came from. She could see nothing, but the noise had seemed louder and more heavy-sounding than anything else she had heard so far and her heart was beating quite breathtakingly hard as she listened. Her eyes flitted anxiously among the surrounding trees, but still found nothing untoward from her place on the bank of the stream.

Then it happened again—a loud cracking sound as if something had trodden on a fallen branch and snapped it, and Delia jumped to her feet, drawing in a sharp breath as she again scanned the trees opposite for some sign of the intruder. Maybe it was some wandering villager in search of kindling and he meant her no harm, but the warnings she had been given would keep coming to mind and she felt quiveringly nervous.

Then, as if making an entrance on to a stage, a large, long-haired goat stepped into the clearing and stood for a second quietly chewing and staring at her with big, pale eyes, only mildly interested. 'Oh, you idiot!' Delia breathed the words aloud and let out a long sigh of relief as she watched the creature move off.

It was another second or two before she realised that in her anxiety to identify the goat she had been careless enough to forget all about her shoes on her lap and she stared down at her bare feet in dismay. Several yards along from where she stood in the water her shoes were racing away on the swift-flowing stream and were already well out of her reach, becoming more impossible to catch every minute.

Instinctively she started forward along the bed of the stream in pursuit, but she already knew it was in vain and she bit her lip in an effort not to cry out when she stubbed her toe on a particularly large stone and winced in pain. Sitting down on the bank again, she nursed her bruised foot and spared only a brief hopeless glance for her vanished shoes. There was nothing for it but a long, painful walk back to the road.

Where it was grassy underfoot she fared comparatively well, but where there were outcrops of rock to contend with the going was not only painful but precarious, for there was the chance of cuts as well as bruises from the rough edges of the rock. It was not sharp rock that caused her downfall, however, but a smooth hump of stone covered in close-growing moss, damp and slippery with the nearness of the running water, and Delia gave a loud cry of distress when her foot suddenly turned sharply and twisted her ankle.

She landed hard upon the ground, her injured leg under her, and tears of pain ran down her cheeks as she took a second to recover her breath before she examined the damage to her foot. She was not very far from the road now, if her estimation was accurate, but as far as she could see she had little hope of going further.

The ankle was swollen and already showing a dark bruise under the throbbing flesh, and Delia looked at it helplessly. She had nothing, not even a handkerchief, to bind it with and it would certainly not support her very far, if at all, but somehow she had to get to the road for there lay her only hope of rescue. Sooner or later someone was bound to come along, even though it might be quite a long wait.

Making her way slowly from tree to tree, she went down the steep incline, grabbing frantically at the rough bark when the gradient threatened to unbalance her. It was a painful and nerve-racking progress and she was crying openly when she at last reached the line of trees that bordered the road.

Sinking down on to the grass bank, she leaned back wearily. Her ankle was throbbing painfully and she was feeling utterly miserable, a small forlorn little figure by the roadside waiting for rescue. There was nothing more she could do but wait.

Delia had no means of telling how long it was before there was any sign of rescue, but she was aware suddenly of the clip-clopping of horses' hooves on the stony road, and raised her head eagerly. A small rough cart appeared around a bend, drawn by a pony, with a woman riding in the back and a man leading the animal; both looked as if they had come from one of the villages, and Delia watched them anxiously as they approached.

The man had fierce black moustaches and wore the rough, simple clothes of a country workman while the woman was dressed in the old style baggy pantaloons worn with an assortment of blouses and over-jackets. The traditional turban-like headcloth she wore was drawn partly across her face as a veil, and two pairs of dark eyes watched Delia curiously as the couple approached.

The little cart came to a halt and the woman got out, pattering along to where Delia sat beside the dusty road. '*Gün aydin, hanim,*' she said in a soft quiet voice but in a dialect so strong that Delia barely recognised even the simple words of greeting. Dark eyes looked down anxiously at her swollen ankle. '*Size yardim edebiliri miyim?*' she asked, but Delia shook her head.

'I'm sorry,' she said huskily. 'I don't speak any Turkish.'

The woman hesitated only a moment, then she indicated by signs that Delia could ride in the cart and the man unhesitatingly nodded agreement. Clinging to the woman's arm, she got to her feet and after a moment the man too came forward and offered his help, bobbing his head slightly as if in apology before putting a strong arm round her waist and half carrying her.

Delia was so intent on gaining the comparative comfort of the cart that she did not even notice the sound of an approaching car until a strident blast on its horn startled both her and her rescuers. Then she raised her head sharply and stared in half dazed surprise, unsure whether to be relieved or dismayed and wondering a little wildly if there was another car on the roads of Turkey besides Kemal Selim's sleek black Mercedes. It always seemed to arrive at awkward times.

He was still wearing the cream suit and brown shirt she had seen him in earlier, but he had dispensed with the tie and his strong brown throat rose from the open neck of the shirt. He parked the car only a few yards away and as he came striding towards them the couple either side of her gently eased Delia on to the bank again and stood back, silently waiting.

There was a taut, almost angry spring in his step that brought a flutter of anxiety to Delia's heartbeat, and she tried to get to her feet again. The move was purely instinctive and simply because she felt more able to face him than she would sitting down, but she realised that it could give quite the wrong impression to the man and his wife.

'Stay where you are!' The order was curt and, Delia thought, impatient, but she obeyed it nevertheless, sinking back on to the grass bank while Kemal went down on one knee beside her. His long, strong fingers took her left foot and examined it, gently considerate of the bruises and the swelling around her ankle, then he looked up at her so swiftly and unexpectedly that she had no time to avoid his gaze. 'Where are your shoes?' he asked, and Delia hesitated.

'I—I dropped them,' she confessed in a small, shaky voice that still held the ghost of a sob. 'They —fell into the water when I stood up.'

He glanced up into the thick crowding trees above them, then back at her. 'You have been up there?' he asked, and Delia nodded without speaking. Anxiety, relief and reaction to her painful journey down the hillside all combined to make her feel completely wretched, and she had never felt less like being cross-questioned by Kemal. He glanced up briefly at her rescuers. 'These people were helping you?' he asked, and again she nodded.

'Yes.'

Kemal got to his feet again and turned to the man and woman, speaking to them at some length in their own tongue. They listened gravely, then both looked at Delia with a curiously speculative expression in their eyes. Eventually, thanks and explanations apparently complete, they took their leave, inclining their heads with grave courtesy before they turned away.

Delia watched them go with mixed feelings, her eyes anxiously flicking back to Kemal as the little cart went on its way down the hill. Kemal, without a word, strode off a few yards along the road and for a heart-stopping moment Delia almost feared he meant to leave her there, but then she saw that he had taken out a big white handkerchief and was dipping it into one of the streams beside the road. Wringing it out, he came back with it to her and once more went down on one knee.

'You had to have your way, *hanim*, hmm?' he asked quietly as he wrapped the cold wet linen round her swollen ankle and tied it securely. 'Now you see what has happened because you chose to disregard advice!'

His touch was gentle and the cold bandage was blessedly soothing, but even so she could not simply sit there and let him scold her like that, and she shook her head firmly. 'It—it was simply bad luck that this happened,' she insisted. 'It had nothing to do with the fact that—that I came here alone.' Her voice trembled alarmingly. 'It could have——'

'It happened, and there was no one there to help you,' Kemal argued quietly. 'If someone had been with you then you would not have lost your shoes!'

'Oh, stop it!' Delia tried to focus her reproachful eyes on him, but reaction told at last and she could see nothing for the haze of tears that blinded her. 'Don't preach at me,' she told him shakily. 'I—I can't do anything to change it now and—and if you—if you don't want——'

'Delia!' She was never quite sure how she came to be in his arms, but he held her close for several seconds while she gave vent to all the frustration and tears that the past hour or so had induced. Her head bowed, her face pressed to the broad comfort of his chest while Kemal's large gentle hand brushed soothingly over her bright hair, she was oblivious of anything but the fact that he was there with her, and it was all that seemed to matter at the moment.

Slowly she raised her head at last and ventured a brief, wary glance at his face. The dark eyes looked down at her, but it was difficult to know what was going on behind them, and his wide straight mouth looked only a little less stern. Putting her hands between them, she pushed herself away, leaving the comforting warmth of his arms while his hands slid with apparent reluctance from her shoulders.

'I'm—I'm sorry,' she whispered huskily, and

sought in vain for a handkerchief.

'You feel better?' Kemal asked, and handed her the twin to the handkerchief that bound her ankle.

Delia gave a long shuddering sigh and nodded her head. 'I—I'm all right, thank you.'

Kemal looked down at her ankle rather pointedly and raised a brow. 'I think that is something of an exaggeration,' he told her coolly, 'and I am in favour of a doctor seeing you in case there is something more than a sprained ankle to be dealt with.'

He got to his feet as if his mind was made up, but Delia looked up at him anxiously. 'Oh no, please,' she begged. 'I'm all right, really, and I don't want to see a doctor!'

'You do not *want*!' Kemal looked at her steadily for a moment as if he meant to insist, but then he shook his head and there was a hint of smile about his mouth as he bent towards her suddenly. 'Very well, *hanim*,' he said, 'since I cannot force you to be sensible, I will take you to your uncle and he will deal with your stubbornness!'

He swept her up into his arms with an ease that took her breath away, and she instinctively slipped an arm round his neck as he carried her to the car. A small pulse throbbed at his temple and there was something disturbingly erotic about that strong column of throat emerging from the open shirt collar that quickened her pulse.

Carefully he placed her in the front seat of the car and his arms slid from around her, then he walked round and slid into the seat beside her. 'I'm—I'm not stubborn,' she ventured as he brought the car engine to life, and Kemal turned his head and looked at her briefly, his eyes unfathomable below heavy lids.

'You are both stubborn and beautiful,' he argued composedly. 'Therefore I shall leave it to your uncle to deal with you!'

Delia looked at the strong, fierce profile with wide eyes and her heart responded like a wild thing to the compliment, however offhand. She leaned back in her seat ready to concede the argument and, despite the throbbing ache in her injured foot, she felt strangely content suddenly.

CHAPTER FIVE

CLIFFORD seemed to take her accident far more to heart than her uncle did, and Delia wondered if the fact that Kemal had been the one to find her was, at least in part, the reason for his concern. When she returned with Kemal he had still been working on the dig and he knew nothing about her being hurt until she appeared at dinner-time with her ankle bandaged and limping, despite Madame Renoir's solicitous support.

Kemal had enrolled his aunt's assistance when Delia still firmly refused to have a doctor called, and Madame Renoir had bathed and quite skilfully bandaged her injured foot with very little comment on the cause. With the possibility in mind of Clifford making a fuss about it Delia had asked that her uncle should not be told until he came back to the house for dinner and, rather surprisingly, Kemal had complied.

She came downstairs on Madame Renoir's supporting arm and met Clifford in the hall, frowning suspiciously when he saw the bandage and the way she was limping. 'What on earth's happened, Delia?' he asked, taking her hand, and Madame Renoir smiled ruefully as she answered for her.

'The poor girl has suffered an injured foot,' she told him, 'but she has been well tended, Monsieur Aitkin, have no fear!'

Smiling her thanks, Delia relinquished the supporting arm in favour of Clifford's and they started slowly across the hall, with Madame Renoir in close attendance. 'I've simply twisted my ankle, Clifford,' she told him. 'It's nothing very terrible, despite the limp!'

Clifford frowned at her anxiously. 'But shouldn't you see a doctor?' he asked. 'I mean, it might be worse than it looks and——'

'It isn't,' Delia insisted, and Madame Renoir smiled at him ruefully.

'We have failed to persuade her, *monsieur*,' she said. 'Kemal was most anxious that she should have a doctor, but Delia will not hear of it!'

He frowned even more doubtfully over the idea of Kemal being involved, but did not comment on it at the moment. 'How did you get back?' he asked.

'You surely didn't walk—where were you?'

'I went up into the forest.'

'After you promised not to? Oh, Delia!' He looked as if he would have continued in that strain, but Delia shook her head firmly.

'I didn't promise,' she denied, 'and—well, something changed my mind and I went.' She glanced at Madame Renoir as if she wondered what she was thinking, but the placid features betrayed nothing. 'It was beautiful,' she went on, determined to stress the good as well as the bad. 'But I lost my shoes in the water, then I turned my ankle.' She laughed a little defiantly, expecting him to take Kemal's view. 'I suppose you could say it was a chapter of accidents!'

'And you walked back barefoot? On an injured ankle?' Clifford looked horrified and she shook her head hastily. 'Then how?'

Once again Delia glanced at Madame Renoir, now walking just slightly in front of them as they slowly crossed the hall. 'I was lucky,' she told Clifford. 'Kemal Bey brought me back and, just as you and Uncle Arthur will no doubt do, he told me it was all my own fault for being so stubborn!'

'Not me!' Clifford denied indignantly. 'I'd hate to think I was so insensitive!' He looked down at her, his grey eyes darkly suspicious behind their lenses. 'But how did he happen to find you?'

Delia explained about the village couple and their offer of help, then smiled up at him. 'Perhaps fortunately, Kemal Bey came along in the car at that moment and spotted me.'

'He always does!' Clifford observed bitterly. 'He always just happens along when you're alone on a country road—I wish I knew how he does it!'

Delia frowned. It was pleasant having a man like Clifford interested in her, flattering too, but he was fast becoming much more possessive than she liked and she wondered how she could tell him so without hurting his feelings. She liked Clifford, he was attractive and he was undoubtedly a good catch for any girl. His interest in archaeology was a hobby rather than a profession and he had wealth enough to indulge it, but Delia was not yet ready to become exclusively interested in him—if she ever did.

'There's really no need for you to sound so—so grumpy about Kemal,' Delia pointed out, taking care to keep her voice low enough for Madame Renoir not to hear. 'It's quite silly of you to let him bother you so when there's no need!'

It was too late for Clifford to make a reply, for they went into the dining salon as she spoke and conversation became general as they joined the others. Delia immediately became the centre of interest, for until now her uncle and their host had known nothing about her being hurt.

Sadi Selim, of course, was sympathetic and most concerned that such a thing should have happened to a guest in his country, solicitous and unfailingly courteous as always. Her uncle, on the other hand, was more inclined to offer criticism of her impatience in not following his advice than sympathy, and Delia did not miss the brief look of satisfaction in Kemal's eyes when he looked at her.

'You really had no need to go up there alone, Delia,' the professor told her reprovingly, and shaking his head he peered at her shortsightedly as they took their places at the table. 'The impatience of young people is beyond belief,' he declared. 'I can't conceive what possessed you to go when you'd been advised not to, Delia.'

Instinctively Delia glanced again at Kemal and this time there was no mistaking the look in his eyes for anything but a certain amused satisfaction. She lowered her own gaze hastily, then as swiftly looked up again when his deep, quiet voice offered an answer to her uncle's query.

'Perhaps I should take some of the fault upon myself, Professor,' he volunteered. 'I offered a challenge to Delia Hanim that she could not resist. That is—' the dark eyes switched briefly back to her—'Delia Hanim read a challenge into a remark of mine and, of course, acted accordingly!'

Delia was unsure whether he was intending to lend his support by sharing the blame, or merely letting them all know that her own stubbornness had led her into going alone simply because of something he had said. Either way his intervention was rather disconcerting and Delia felt strangely uneasy with all eyes on her.

Clifford especially would dislike any suggestion of Kemal's involvement and he was frowning at her already, his eyes suspicious. 'Is it true, Delia?' he asked, and Delia hesitated only briefly before she answered him.

'I suppose so,' she admitted, but left no doubt

that she resented being questioned about it. Her eyes were on Kemal rather than Clifford and her chin defied him to complicate matters further.

Clifford looked not only puzzled but disapproving, even before he knew the facts. 'But why, for heaven's sake?' he asked, and Delia shrugged.

'Maybe because I hadn't any more sense,' she told him a little impatiently, then glanced swiftly at Kemal again. 'Or maybe because I'm as donkey-stubborn as Kemal Bey tells me I am!'

Sadi Selim looked up sharply, his fierce black eyes narrowed when he looked at his grandson, and it was obvious that only his unfailing courtesy prevented him from questioning Kemal there and then about her meaning. Kemal himself looked less perturbed than anyone and he looked across at her with a bright dark glitter in his eyes that recognised her jibe for what it was.

'Delia Hanim quotes me out of context and inaccurately,' he said quietly, 'as I am sure she will admit.'

For a moment Delia refused to co-operate, but then, moved by something she did not quite understand, she smiled at the old man and shook her head. 'I'm sorry if I gave the wrong impression, Sadi Bey,' she told him. 'Kemal Bey's opinion was a little more politely worded.' She laughed softly and looked at Sadi Selim with a hint of mischief in her eyes. 'Anyway,' she added, 'he's probably right!'

'Of course he's right!' her uncle declared firmly, and Delia wrinkled her nose at him and smiled. Kemal, she noticed from the corner of her eye, was already getting on with his meal as if he had no doubts at all about his veracity.

Clifford should have already joined the professor on the site, but somehow this morning he seemed disinclined to leave her and Delia was certainly not averse to his company at the moment. Her ankle was still quite painful and she had been advised by Madame Renoir to rest for at least another day or two, but the idea of being confined to the house did not altogether appeal to Delia in her present restless mood, especially on her own.

'I could stay with you this morning,' Clifford offered hopefully, but Delia shook her head.

He was sitting on one of the floor cushions beside her and, dressed as he was, he looked very much out of place in this big exotic room. Faded shorts and a cotton shirt suggested English country rambles, but the salon was, to Delia's mind, the most completely Turkish room in the house. It was because he looked so alien to his surroundings that she felt a sudden inexplicable tenderness towards him, and reached out to put a hand on his arm. 'I'd love you to stay,' she told him, 'but Uncle Arthur would soon be up here if you did, demanding to know why you're not working, and I'm already sufficiently in his bad books after yesterday.'

Clifford looked at her bandaged ankle and it was obvious that he had something to say about yesterday's incident that he had so far had no opportunity to say. 'I don't think he should blame you entirely,' he told her. 'Selim admitted that he——'

'Kemal was simply trying to explain why I went out after all,' she interrupted hastily. 'I went out of my own accord, Clifford, and I've no one else I can blame.'

For a moment Clifford said nothing. He sat with his knees supporting his elbows and there was such a look of uncertainty about him that Delia wondered what on earth he had in mind. 'He—Selim —seems to—to know you so much better than I do,' he said, then waved his hands vaguely to erase the statement. 'No—no, that's not what I mean exactly,' he denied. 'It's just that he seems to have the ability to—to *get* to you!' Delia looked puzzled and slightly taken aback and he shook his head again. 'I mean,' he explained, 'that he at least arouses *some* kind of—of reaction in you, whereas——' He shrugged, a strangely touching gesture of helplessness that she could not ignore, 'you take me as part of the scenery.'

'Oh, Clifford, that's simply not true!'

Delia curled both her hands round his arm, seeking to reassure him. 'Isn't it?' he asked, and she smiled, gently squeezing his arm.

'No, of course not! You should know that, Clifford!'

Clifford responded to the gesture by moving quickly towards her, sliding from his own cushion on to hers, and his grey eyes glowed with an inner warmth as he put an arm around her waist. It became apparent as soon as he spoke that her impulsive gesture of encouragement had been taken in quite the wrong way, and she would have drawn back hastily if such a manoeuvre had been possible in the space.

'Oh, Delia!' His voice was husky with emotion and he took her hand in his, pressing it to his lips, then hugging her close in an embrace that her injured foot made it impossible to avoid. 'You know how I feel about you, Delia, don't you?' he begged. 'I've loved you ever since I met you at the professor's house last summer!'

'Clifford!' She moved away as far as she could get without toppling over on to the floor, but Clifford drew her close again, holding her more tightly and reaching round with his other arm to complete an inescapable circle around her. 'Clifford, I didn't mean you to—to react like this!' She wriggled in vain, trying to escape, but Clifford's grey eyes were bright and determined as he looked down at her. 'Clifford, please!'

He held her tightly, murmuring her name and soft, irresistible pleas that undermined her resistance, so that eventually she offered little opposition when he kissed her. It was a light, tentative kiss, though firm enough to be sincere, but it was nothing like Kemal's fierce, sensual passion, and it was Kemal's kiss that came to mind as she closed her eyes, making her try once again to break free.

It was while she was struggling against Clifford's determination that she realised the door of the salon had opened and that they were no longer alone. Without turning around, Delia's instinct told her who it was and she turned swiftly and gazed at him with wide, slightly dazed eyes.

'I am sorry to intrude,' Kemal said, pedantically correct as always. He spared her only a brief glance, then gave his attention to Clifford. 'Professor Crompton asks that you report to the site, Mr. Aitkin,' he told him. 'However, if you would like a message sent——' His dark eyes flicked again to Delia and one brow expressed his meaning quite clearly. 'You would like him told that you are otherwise engaged, perhaps?' he suggested.

Flushed and embarrassed, Clifford scrambled to his feet. 'Not at all!' he said, and rubbed a hand through his slightly disordered hair while his eyes carefully avoided looking at either Delia or Kemal. 'I was on my way, as a matter of fact.'

'Ah!' The brief exclamation could have expressed satisfaction and Kemal inclined his head briefly, then walked over to the window and stood with his back to them.

Clifford, evidently expecting him to leave again, seemed taken aback when he stayed and looked as if he wondered what to do. Then he looked down at Delia with a kind of hesitant confidence in his eyes. 'I wish I could stay, Delia,' he said in a quiet, half whispering voice. 'Please believe me.'

'I do!' She smiled at him, much more disturbed by Kemal's arrival than by Clifford's imminent departure.

'Promise me you won't do anything else silly while I'm gone?' The hint of possessiveness in his tone was not altogether welcome and she glanced at Kemal instinctively.

He stood at the window, tall and somehow

slightly menacing with his back towards them, his lean, powerful shape dark against the bright sunlight outside, and it was obvious that he had no intention of going. Then suddenly Clifford bent over her and, before she realised his intent, took her face in his two hands and kissed her mouth. 'I'll see you later,' he whispered.

There was a suggestion of subterfuge in his manner that was completely without cause, and as she watched him go with slightly dazed eyes, Delia wondered if there had ever been two men under one roof who were so completely unalike. Clifford, only medium tall and so very English in his faded shorts and shirt, and Kemal, dark and sultry, his tailoring as impeccable as his manners, and yet still capable of conveying his opinion of the scene he had interrupted.

It was his impression of that scene that troubled Delia, although heaven knew why she should bother what he thought. She looked across at the broad back, a jacket of fawn tussore stretched across the breadth of his shoulders, and the dark head held so arrogantly on the strong neck. A virile and powerful man who could cause havoc to any woman's senses, and especially a susceptible girl thrown into his company every day.

He turned swiftly and suddenly from the window and Delia hastily looked away, although she was aware of the scrutiny of those dark eyes for several seconds before he spoke. 'How is your injured ankle this morning, *hanim*?' he asked, and Delia frowned unconsciously over the formality of the title.

'It's painful,' she said, 'but Madame Renoir suggests I rest it for a couple of days.'

'Then that is what you should do,' Kemal advised gravely. He would have said more, Delia thought, but the door opened once more and one of the servants announced the arrival of a caller.

If the identity of the caller caused Kemal a puzzled frown, it stunned Delia into disbelief, but when the visitor was admitted to the salon she had to believe that Suna Kozlu had taken the unprecedented step of calling unaccompanied on a man in his home. Delia's heart was fluttering uneasily and when Kemal went forward to welcome the visitor she felt suddenly and dismayingly intrusive.

Impulsively she scrambled to her feet, made clumsy by her bandaged foot, and stood for a moment looking at the two of them together, exchanging rather stilted greetings. They did not shake hands, neither did they embrace, but they looked so right somehow, Delia had to admit. Two darkly attractive people with the same background of race and culture and heaven knew what else in common—it was a fact, palatable or not, that Suna Kozlu would be the perfect wife for Kemal.

'You have met Miss Crompton, have you not?' Kemal asked, turning to include Delia, and Suna Kozlu inclined her head gravely, though it was obvious she had not expected to find her there.

'*Gün aydin, hanim,*' she said. There was a dark, wary look in her eyes as she spoke and they missed nothing of Delia's red-gold hair and slim, petite figure, nor the bandage that bound her ankle. 'You have suffered an injury?' she enquired politely.

Unsure just where explanations could lead her, Delia decided to treat the matter lightly. 'I turned my ankle, that's all,' she said. 'It's nothing serious, Miss Kozlu.'

The dark, not altogether friendly, eyes regarded her for a moment as if the consequences of an injured ankle did not escape her. 'So you are confined to the house?' she guessed, and flicked a brief but telling glance at Kemal. 'How tiresome for you, *hanim*!'

She was jealous of the idea of her being in such close contact with Kemal, Delia thought wildly, and her own pulses acknowledged the possibilities it offered as Kemal's dark eyes glittered down at her. 'Perhaps you can persuade Delia Hanim to take care of the injury, Suna,' he suggested quietly. 'I am afraid that such advice from us merely meets with a determination not to follow it—as you are a doctor perhaps your word will carry more weight!'

It was debatable who was most surprised by the suggestion, but Suna Kozlu recovered her composure first and when she looked at Delia again there was no concealing the glint of dislike in her dark eyes. 'I am not yet a doctor, *hanim*,' she told her, 'but I am sufficiently trained to know that it is essential to rest such an injury if it is to recover.'

'I—I *do* realise that, of course,' Delia admitted, and glanced uneasily at Kemal. She wanted nothing so much as to escape and leave them together, but it was not easy in the circumstances, for Kemal at least seemed intent on including her in the conversation.

'To rest means to sit down again, Delia Hanim,' he told her, but Delia shook her head urgently, resolved to follow her own inclination.

'Not at the moment,' she murmured huskily. 'If you'll excuse me I—I'll leave you.' She would have made it to the door, but as she passed him Kemal laid a hand on her arm, a gesture that the visitor noted with a quick frown.

'There is no need for you to leave,' he said quietly, and Delia stared at him, unable to understand his motives for the moment. It took a second or two for it to occur to her that perhaps he wanted her to stay to satisfy his taste for tradition—so that he and Suna Kozlu would not be alone.

The very thought of his thinking of her as some kind of youthful chaperone made her suddenly angry and she snatched her arm from his hold, casting a brief glance at Suna Kozlu as she hobbled her way to the door. 'I'd rather leave, Kemal Bey, if you don't mind,' she told him in a voice that was as firm as she could make it. 'Please excuse me, Miss Kozlu!'

The Turkish girl inclined her head politely, but it was plain that she found Delia's departure, although to her own liking, not only unexpected but puzzling; as if she could not believe Delia would willingly leave her alone with Kemal. Having escaped from an embarrassing situation Delia stood for a few seconds on the other side of the door, trying to do something about the rapid and anxious beat of her heart. She was certainly not prepared to stay and play chaperone to Suna Kozlu and Kemal, and the idea of his expecting her to not only made her angry but rather surprisingly hurt too.

It was close on ten minutes since Delia had heard Suna Kozlu's car depart, but she had made no attempt to return to the house. A short turn round the garden had made her dismayingly tired and her foot throbbed painfully so that she sat for a while on a low wall that surrounded a raised bed spilling over with sweetly scented lilies and roses. A tall, dark-plumed cypress gave her shade from the sun and she was thoughtfully preoccupied as she sat with her feet dangling just above the ground.

She had no idea why Suna Kozlu had come to Mavisu, nor should it concern her, but somehow the fact that she had come was strangely disturbing, and nothing could dispel the curiosity she felt. It was true that Suna Kozlu was a product of modern Turkey, an emancipated woman who wanted to be a doctor and who had, if Madame Renoir and Kemal's implications were right, refused to give up the idea for marriage.

But it was also possible that meeting Kemal again in the restaurant had brought about a change of heart, and it was that possibility that sat so uncomfortably in Delia's mind. That Suna Kozlu had come to Mavisu with the idea of letting Kemal know how she felt, even though she might draw the line at actually telling him so. Kemal would not be slow to realise her intent if that was the case, Delia felt sure of it.

'So—once again you go against good advice, *hanim!*' Kemal's deep voice from behind her made Delia swing round sharply and she fought for a second with the uncontrollable beating of her heart.

'I'm not likely to come to any harm out here in the garden,' she told him, and Kemal raised a doubting brow.

He came and stood close beside her and she despaired of the way her whole being responded to his nearness. One hand was thrust into a pocket and his jacket swung open, revealing a fine white shirt through which the shadowy darkness of his body showed faintly. It was difficult not to recognise and be affected by the sheer strength and vigour of the man behind that formally polite exterior, and Delia curled her hands tightly as she looked up at him.

'I cannot believe that it is good for an injured foot to be suspended in that way,' he declared firmly. 'It should be resting on a cushion, *hanim*, as you had it earlier. There was really no need for you to leave in the way you did.'

Delia looked at him warily, too unsure of her ground to be too hasty, then she shook her head. 'I'm not in the habit of intruding into other people's private conversations, Kemal Bey,' she told him. 'I could hardly stay when you and Miss Kozlu had——' She shrugged off possible topics of conversation he might share with his visitor. 'I might warrant being called stubborn, but never tactless!'

For a moment he said nothing, and she curled her hands even more tightly as she waited. Then he put one foot on the low wall beside her and rested an elbow on his knee, looking down at her steadily. 'And you consider I was—tactless to walk into the salon when you and Mr. Aitkin were——' Expressive hands made a great deal of Clifford's diffident kiss, and Delia flushed, her eyes bright and sparkling green as she looked up at him.

'Clifford kissed me,' she told him a little breathlessly, 'but you can hardly claim to be shocked by that, Kemal Bey, since you've done the same yourself! Just as then, it signified absolutely nothing!'

'Ah!' Yet again he made that curiously expressive sound that could cover all manner of meanings, and Delia despaired of ever understanding him.

'I rather thought you and Miss Kozlu might have things to say that you'd rather not say with a third party present,' she went on recklessly, 'and even if you hadn't I had no desire to—to chaperone you!'

She half expected him to be angry, but there was no sign of it beyond that deep, dark gleam in his eyes and he still rested his elbow on a raised knee, looking down at her steadily. 'Whatever reason you have for supposing Suna Kozlu called to see me,' he told her in a calm, composed voice, 'I can assure you that it was of no more consequence than to return a fountain pen that I left at her home yesterday.'

'It doesn't concern me!'

She was finding it hard to think straight at the

moment. Not only was he much too close for comfort but she now knew where he had been yesterday
when he came along and rescued her, and she
almost wished she had not found out. Their attach-
ment must be every bit as close as she suspected,
more seriously intent on marriage, or Kemal with
his traditionalist ideas would never have called on
Suna Kozlu at her home.

'You seem angry, *hanim*,' Kemal suggested, and
Delia looked up quickly to deny it, then as quickly
looked away again. One large hand slid beneath her
chin before she could evade it and strong fingers
dug firmly into her soft flesh as he held her. 'And
why should you be angry?' he asked softly.

The touch of his hand made her pulses stir
rapidly in response and the sense of excitement she
experienced was breathtaking. Her lips parted
slightly as she fought with her chaotic senses, her
eyes wide and uncertain as she looked up at him.
'I—I'm not angry,' she denied huskily, and his
thumb moved gently over her parted lips in a suggestive caress that made her head spin.

'No?' he asked softly. Then, as if he suddenly
recalled himself, he relinquished his hold on her
and shook his head, looking down at her with a hint
of smile on his stern mouth. 'But I must not allow
you to stay here like this when you should be resting
your injured foot,' he told her. 'I will take you back
to the salon.'

Deprived of that seductive touch on her mouth
Delia felt strangely let down, almost as if he had
been deliberately tantalising her for his own amuse-

ment, and she was instinctively on the defensive. 'I don't want to go back to the salon!' she argued. 'And I wish you wouldn't concern yourself with me, Kemal Bey. I'm perfectly capable of deciding whether I'm doing the right thing or not!'

Whatever Kemal said was in Turkish, but it sounded as virulent as curses in any language and his raised foot thudded on to the ground beside her. She gave a soft cry of surprise when she was lifted into his arms suddenly and without warning, but her arms went naturally to encircle his neck.

She was held close to the warm, angry tautness of his body and the strong steady beat of his heart throbbed against her own body like a drum beat. His arms were hard and unyielding and there was a rocklike sternness about his mouth and chin when she chanced a brief upward glance. That tangy, masculine scent she remembered affected her senses like wine and she clung to him tightly while he strode across the scented gardens with her.

The door of the salon was already open and he took her in there and set her down on one of the cushions with unexpected gentleness, although there was nothing suggestive of gentleness in the fierce dark eyes that looked down at her a moment later. 'If you wish to prove how stubborn you can be,' he said in a deep, scornful voice, 'you are doing exactly that! For my part I cannot believe that anyone, even you, *hanim*, can be so foolish as to retard their own recovery simply to exhibit defiance!'

Much as she disliked admitting it, Delia was

obliged to some extent to see his point of view, but she felt rather small and vulnerable suddenly now that she sat at his feet. Her flesh still retained the warmth of his body and she felt strangely bereft without its tingling contact so that she looked up at him with a faintly appealing look in her green eyes that she was quite unaware of.

'I—I wish you wouldn't call me *hanim*,' she said in a small voice, and Kemal narrowed his eyes for a moment before he answered.

'It is the correct form of address for a woman,' he reminded her after a few seconds, and she wondered if she imagined the more gentle note in his voice.

'But only when you want to be very formal,' she ventured, her heart beating anxiously hard. 'With women you don't know very well or——' She hesitated and hastily looked down at her hands. 'And you don't always use it, do you?'

Again he studied her for several seconds, and he looked so tall and fierce that she wondered why she was not afraid of him. Then he sat down suddenly in one swift easy movement, his legs crossed in the traditional posture, on the cushion next to hers. Unhurriedly he took out a case and extracted a long flat cigarette from it, his strong fingers fascinating in their dexterity as he lit it and expelled a long plume of blue smoke from his lips.

'Perhaps I should call you *bebek* instead,' he suggested with a hint of smile behind the concealing smoke. 'It would perhaps be more appropriate, although less complimentary.'

'*Bebek?*' She echoed the strange word, looking

puzzled, and his eyes glittered with malicious amusement as he looked at her steadily.

'Baby,' he translated obligingly, and Delia flushed.

'I see!' She would have liked to get to her feet and walk out of the room had it not been for the effort involved, instead she glared at him indignantly and lifted her chin. 'I fail to see why you see me as a baby simply because I don't like taking orders,' she told him, and refused to be warned by the slight narrowing of his eyes. 'But I suppose Turkish women are accustomed to being treated like second-class citizens and you think I should be grateful to you!'

Even before she had finished speaking she could have bitten out her tongue, but it was too late now and Kemal's strong right hand was already crushing out the cigarette with a slow force so suggestive of violence that she shivered. He got to his feet and did not even look at her, but turned his back as if she was beneath his notice, and strode off.

Delia watched him, her heart thudding relentlessly hard in her breast, then, spurred by heaven knew what compulsion, she called after him. 'I'm sorry!' Her voice sounded so small and uncertain that she scarcely recognised it, but she thought he hesitated. 'Please,' she insisted, encouraged by that slight hesitation. 'I really am sorry, Kemal Bey!'

He turned, slowly, his dark eyes shadowed by half lowered lids, and for a moment she almost expected him to curse her, but then he strode back across the room in great long strides that brought him back to her much sooner than she expected, so that she caught her breath when he dropped down on to the cushion she sat on, facing her and so close their bodies touched.

He gave her no time to say or do anything, but reached for her with his hands and pulled her into his arms, pressing her so hard against him that she let out a faint cry of surprise. The softness of the cushion yielded to their combined weights and his body forced her to sink back, her arms once more going instinctively around his neck while his mouth sought hers with a passionate fierceness that blotted out everything else but the urgent desires of her own senses.

There was a fierceness in his kiss, a suppressed violence that suggested he was still angry, but there was also an irresistible hunger in the mouth that parted her lips with its force and it was that she responded to so eagerly. On the brink of complete surrender to her own desires, she was made aware of some alien sound in the big room, some distant voice that dragged her back from ecstasy.

She fought hard for a moment against the arms that bound her and managed at last to turn her head, breathing erratically as she gazed with unseeing eyes at the slowly closing door. Turning again, she looked up into Kemal's face, and shivered at the look of dark passion that still lingered there.

Her lips were warm and still tingled with his kiss and she looked up at him in silence for a moment before she found her voice. 'Some—someone came in,' she whispered, and noticed dazedly how quickly he frowned. Then his eyes searched her face slowly, as if he was seeing her for the first time, his hands still holding her, his body still pressing her back into the softness of the cushion.

'That troubles you?' he suggested softly, but gave her no time to confirm or deny it. He eased himself upright and sat for a moment on the cushion beside her, then reaching down he drew her into a sitting position and held her for a moment before dropping his hands from her arms. 'Of course it troubles you,' he said, answering his own question, 'and I can only express my regret once again, Delia, for having——' his big hands spread meaningly. 'What can I say?' he asked.

Delia shook her head, only now beginning to wonder who it was who had so discreetly closed the door again and left them. Sadi Selim would have been scandalised at such a scene and Clifford would certainly have made his presence known, so that left only her uncle and Madame Renoir, and of those two Delia thought the little Frenchwoman was the most likely.

'Don't—don't say anything,' she begged, and looked for a moment at the strong, dark profile outlined against the window and the broad hands that were clasped together though showing no sign of tension. 'I—I suppose I was partly to blame,' she ventured in a small husky voice, and Kemal turned his head slowly and looked at her, one brow raised, then his straight mouth twitched into the ghost of a smile.

'Would it be ungallant of me to agree with you?'

he asked quietly, and Delia blinked at him for a moment, uncertain what to say.

'Perhaps not,' she whispered.

Kemal got up suddenly, standing over her for a moment, his dark eyes unfathomable in the cool shadowy salon. Then he reached down for her hand and quite unexpectedly raised it to his lips. 'Try not to tempt me too often, *bebek*,' he said in a soft deep voice. 'I am too much a man to be able to resist you!'

Her heart racing wildly, every nerve tingling, Delia watched him go, striding on long legs to the door—and he was gone before she could think of a reason for calling him back.

CHAPTER SIX

CLIFFORD had driven into Antalya during the morning for something the professor needed for the dig, but it was not until he mentioned the fact to Delia after lunch that she reminded him that she would have enjoyed the drive in with him. 'Of course I could have taken you,' he admitted, 'but quite honestly I didn't give it a thought, Delia. The professor was in such a hurry and I simply didn't stop to think about anything else.'

'Not even me,' Delia complained ruefully.

Clifford took her hands in his, squeezing her fingers gently. 'I'm sorry, my dear,' he said contritely. 'I didn't really forget you, of course, but the professor gave me no time to think—you know how impatient he always is when he wants anything.'

Delia looked at him and smiled, obliged to recognise the truth of that. 'I know,' she acknowledged. 'He really has no right to call *me* impatient!'

Clifford leaned forward and kissed her lightly on her cheek. 'I'll take you out again, Delia,' he whispered, resting his forehead against hers and looking down at her, 'I promise I will, as soon as the professor gives me another free day, although heaven knows when that will be. Everything's going so well at the moment—we've uncovered almost the entire stereobate now, the substructure of the temple, and we can see the layout as a whole!'

His enthusiasm was as great as her uncle's and quite understandable, but Delia recognised that everything and everybody would have to take second place to his first love, no matter what protestations he made, and she smiled a little ruefully. There was a slightly breathless sound to his voice and his eyes gleamed, but while she acknowledged the reason for his exhilaration she could not share in it to the same degree.

'It's very exciting,' she agreed. 'I only wish I could be there.'

'Oh, but of course you can't, darling, I understand that,' Clifford denied, and she swallowed hard on the unfamiliar use of the endearment. 'It wouldn't be safe for you to be hobbling about on the uneven ground with that ankle, but *I* wish you could be with us too!' He looked at her bandaged foot, very much less swollen but still painful when she put her weight on it. 'How much better is it after a rest?' he asked.

'Much better than it was,' Delia told him, but he frowned.

'I wish you'd have a doctor to see it, Delia,' he said. 'You'd probably be up and around much quicker if you had proper treatment and I'd feel much happier about it.'

'It certainly isn't worth troubling a doctor with it now,' she insisted. 'If I thought it would make a difference to the time I have to spend resting it, I'd see a doctor, but there's no point when I'm just sitting here anyway.'

'Missing all the fun,' Clifford suggested, and squeezed her fingers again. 'Poor Delia!'

'I suppose I can't complain too much,' she admitted with a smile. 'But I do like to know what's going on.'

Clifford looked as if he just remembered something, and he raised her fingers to his mouth and kissed them lightly, not looking at her as he spoke. 'I saw Selim while I was in Antalya,' he told her, and something in his voice, some note of harshness, suggested he had something more to say on the matter.

She tried to do something about the rapid beating of her heart as she sought to steady her voice.

She made no pretence of suggesting he referred to the old man, for Clifford always used Sadi Selim's full name. Only Kemal merited that rather derisive abbreviation. 'They have some business interests, I believe,' she ventured. 'It was probably in connection with that he was there.'

'I hardly think so!' Clifford declared, and there was a gleam in his eyes she did not care for, though she tried not to let the depth of her interest show. 'He was talking to a woman in the car park near the bus station,' he went on. 'A tallish, rather attractive girl, obviously Turkish.'

Recognising the description all too easily, Delia was appalled to realise how much she hated learning about Kemal's latest meeting with Suna Kozlu, but she did her best to seem no more than casually interested. 'Oh, that will have been Suna Kozlu,' she told Clifford. 'She was here yesterday just after you left me—she came to see Kemal.'

'*Did* she?' It was plain from his raised brows that Clifford put much the same construction on the visit as Delia had herself, and was just as surprised by it. 'I thought Selim was a traditionalist,' he remarked, pursing his lips on possible implications. 'You know—keep the women in their place and all that. This girl looked very modern and emancipated, there was nothing suggestive of—of the harem about *her*!'

'Why should there be? They don't have harems any more, as you well know!' Delia told him, trying hard to concentrate on answering Clifford rather than on the reasons Kemal had gone into Antalya to meet Suna Kozlu. 'Miss Kozlu's training to be a doctor,' she added. 'I believe she qualifies next year.'

Clifford looked at her curiously. 'You've met her?' he asked, and Delia nodded.

'Twice, actually. Yesterday was the second time.' She fought hard to be fair about her impression of Suna Kozlu. 'She's—she's very pleasant.'

'Hmm!' Clifford still looked thoughtful, as if the existence of Suna Kozlu gave him food for thought. Then he looked at Delia for a second or two with slightly narrowed eyes. 'Is it possible he's serious about this lady doctor?' he asked, and Delia curled her hands tightly.

'How on earth would I know?' she demanded shortly.

Clifford pondered the idea further, one elbow resting on his knee. 'It's possible, of course, that she's just——' His shrug was almost as expressive as one of Madame Renoir's and Delia found it hard to attribute such worldly ideas to Clifford. 'I imagine men like Selim still *think* in terms of a harem, even if they aren't legal any more,' he said, and Delia frowned.

'Oh, you're just being—biased about it,' she declared without stopping to think what he could make of her swift defence of Kemal. 'How can you know what Kemal or anyone else feels, Clifford?'

'Sorry!' The apology was short and ungracious, and his grey eyes had a bright, angry look that she had seen there once before, and that time too they had been discussing Kemal Selim. He looked at her for a moment narrowly, his mouth too expressing the dislike he felt for her attitude. 'It just seems to me,' he said after a second or two, 'that the old rules allowed a man to have his cake and eat it too, and Kemal Selim is the type who'd do just that, given half a chance!'

It was difficult for Delia to know how to answer him, for when she considered the events of the past few days it could be said that Kemal had been indulging himself rather in the way that Clifford suggested. He had been with Suna Kozlu three times to Delia's knowledge, and he had kissed Delia herself in a way that certainly did not suggest he thought of her as a baby, even though he had called her one. Finding the possible truth too discomfiting, she shrugged uneasily and refused to look at Clifford when she spoke.

'It doesn't concern me what Kemal does,' she told him in a voice that was dismayingly hard to control. 'And I'd be glad if you'd change the subject, Clifford.'

'Of course, darling!' He leaned forward again and kissed her, then glanced at his wristwatch and pulled a rueful face. 'I'll have to leave you,' he said, 'much as I hate to, Delia, but I'll sound out the professor this afternoon and see if he'll let me have at least another half day off, perhaps tomorrow.'

'It would be nice to go out somewhere,' Delia said, feeling quite sorry for herself as he got to his feet. 'I get a bit fed up sitting around!'

'Poor darling!' Clifford bent again and kissed her lightly. 'I'll be back to see you as soon as I can!'

Clifford had been gone no more than ten minutes when Kemal came into the salon and Delia felt the swift colour in her cheeks when he looked across at her and half smiled, his wide straight mouth suggesting that he knew Clifford had been obliged to leave her.

It was discomfiting to have him come in so soon after she had been discussing him with Clifford, and she hoped that if he stayed she could exert more control over the situation than she had yesterday. He seemed in no hurry to leave, but took a cigarette from a box standing on one of the numerous small tables in the room.

Once again she watched those long, strong fingers with an almost hypnotic fascination and despaired of her own weakness. The long, lean body, its sensual vigour only partially civilised by a formal suit in light grey and a white shirt, leaned above the small table, then straightened slowly as he turned his head and looked across at her. He wore no tie and his brown throat had a small pulse at its base that throbbed steadily; his eyes narrowed against the rising smoke, dark and unfathomable, looked at her steadily for several seconds, then briefly he smiled.

'You are feeling sorry for yourself?' he guessed, and Delia instinctively lifted her chin in dissent.

'Not at all!' she denied, her voice not quite steady. 'I've been talking to Clifford, he's only just left me.'

'Ah!' That short, expressive sound seemed to serve him in all manner of ways, but usually it conveyed satisfaction, she thought. 'Then he cannot spend the afternoon with you as he had hoped, hmm?'

Delia shook her head. 'He's working,' she told him, 'as I should be if it wasn't for this wretched ankle. They're getting on wonderfully well, so in the circumstances, there's not much hope of Clifford being spared for some time now.'

'So you are left to pine alone while your goddess has everyone's attention, huh?'

Delia looked at him curiously. '*My* goddess?' she asked, and Kemal smiled, shaking his head.

'You are the archaeologist, Delia Hanim,' he said. 'Surely you are aware of the connection between yourself and Artemis, are you not?'

Delia frowned, completely foxed for the moment. Way back in her childhood she remembered being told something about her name being mythical in origin, but both her father and her uncle's interests had always been in the more human side of archaeology and the mythical legends were only vaguely familiar to her.

'I don't claim to be an archaeologist,' she denied, 'but I believe my name does have some significance, although I can't remember if I ever knew exactly what it was.'

Kemal's dark eyes glowed in a way that made her tremble despite the hint of mockery in his smile. 'And I thought you a romantic,' he said. 'Yet you do not know the connection between yourself and the goddess Artemis whose temple you have discovered!'

'A romantic?' She looked at him uncertainly for a moment, unsure how true it was, then after a moment she glanced down instead at her clasped hands. 'I—I suppose I am,' she said. 'At least I find the old legends very interesting, although I confess I don't know a lot about Artemis.'

One dark brow arched curiously and he sent another spiral of blue smoke drifting like a screen before his face. 'May I presume to lecture you?' he asked and, when she nodded silently, he sat himself in the armchair facing her and crossed one long leg over the other. 'You know that the Greek goddess Artemis was known to the Romans as Diana?'

'Yes, I did know that,' Delia admitted, fascinated by the fact that he seemed far more knowledgeable than she had expected. She looked at him briefly again from the corners of her eyes. 'Are you interested in archaeology, Kemal Bey?' she asked.

'A basic knowledge only,' Kemal confessed. 'Along this coast it is almost impossible not to acquire a certain amount of intelligence on the subject of the old gods, Delia Hanim, as you will appreciate.'

'Yes, yes, of course.'

Once more his features were obscured by a cloud of smoke from pursed lips. His elbow rested on the arm of his chair and he seemed relaxed and completely at ease in contrast to her own rather disordered thoughts. 'To return to your own connection with the goddesses,' he said, 'the Roman Diana was reputed to have been born on the island of Delos in the Aegean, not very far from here, and from the island name comes your own—Delia. So you see why I refer to her as your goddess?'

Delia nodded, but she found it hard to concentrate on goddesses, no matter how closely connected with herself. Kemal was much too close for comfort and his quiet composure served only to remind her of his passion yesterday. It seemed incredible that he could sit there facing her and talk so calmly about the old gods, when yesterday he had kissed her in such a way that she had felt herself transported to another world.

She licked her lips anxiously and kept her eyes on her clasped hands, conscious of him watching her through that concealing haze of cigarette smoke. 'I believe—I think I did hear that when I was little,' she told him, 'but I'd forgotten until you reminded me.'

'Has Mr. Aitkin not reminded you?' Kemal asked softly, and Delia glanced up quickly, wondering why he should suddenly see fit to mention Clifford again.

Shaking her head, she frowned at him curiously. 'No,' she said, 'he hasn't—but there's no real reason why he should, is there?'

Kemal's broad shoulders shrugged with deceptive carelessness as he again drew on the cigarette. 'I would find the temptation to compare my—*kiz* to a goddess irresistible,' he confessed, and the dark eyes glittered at her from behind the smoke screen. 'But perhaps Mr. Aitkin prefers his goddesses of cool stone, hmm?' he suggested softly, and Delia flushed.

'If—*kiz* means what I think it does,' she said huskily, 'I—I'm not, whatever it is, to Clifford and you have no right to suggest I am!'

'Ah!' Once again that brief, satisfied sound conveyed his meaning, and she shook her head, so uncertain that she could only gaze at him anxiously. 'But he does not, I think, prefer stone goddesses, eh, *bebek*?'

'I don't know what he prefers!' Delia curled her hands tightly, her heart anxiously thudding a warning that yet again she was heading for an argument with Kemal that could lead heaven knew where.

He said nothing for a moment but regarded her steadily with those unfathomable eyes as he reached over and extinguished his cigarette. When he got up he stood for a moment looking down at her, disconcertingly close, studying her as if he only now recognised some new aspect of her. 'And you do not care?' he suggested.

Delia could have denied it, but she did not see why she should justify herself to him. 'Not particularly!' she said.

Still Kemal studied her with that quiet intensity, his eyes darkly disturbing. 'You can be cruel, Delia Hanim,' he said coldly. 'I count myself fortunate not to be in the shoes of Clifford Aitkin!'

Too stunned for the moment to say anything, even in her own defence, Delia stared at him. The frank opinion was both harsh and unexpected and for the life of her she could not see that she had said or done anything to deserve it. Perhaps she had been a little too hasty in her reply, but she had spoken without thinking and more to defy him than to denigrate Clifford.

'Cruel?' She echoed the accusation while her eyes still watched him dazedly. 'How can you say that? What—what makes you say it?'

A hint of smile touched his wide straight mouth for a moment and he regarded her steadily without speaking, then he shook his head slowly. 'You really do not know that man, do you?' he asked. 'He does not—touch you, here!' He struck his own broad chest with one hand and shook his head.

Delia blinked, her brain racing. How could he claim to sympathise with Clifford when to all appearances he did not even like him? Anxiously she licked her dry lips and shook her head. 'You—you don't understand,' she said in a small husky voice. 'Clifford——' She turned sharply when the door opened and almost sighed her relief aloud when Madame Renoir walked in.

Bright dark eyes flicked from one to the other and a raised brow questioned the reason for Delia's flushed cheeks and Kemal's position beside her. 'I did not know you were here, *mon cher* Kemal,' she told him, and for one insane moment Delia wondered if she was going to offer to leave again.

Kemal inclined his head briefly, then smiled. 'I would have left a few moments ago, Tante Yvette,' he acknowledged, 'but I have plenty of time.'

'So you came to cheer Delia, hmm?' Madame Renoir suggested blandly. 'I am sure your thoughtfulness was welcome, *mon cher*!'

Kemal fixed her with a steady unavoidable gaze

and Delia tried hard to look away. There was a hint of challenge in the depth of his eyes that she was all too familiar with. 'I am not so sure,' he said quietly, 'but I am sure you will meet with a warmer welcome, Tante Yvette!'

'You cannot be serious!' Madame Renoir smiled at Delia. 'Tell him how wrong he is, Delia, huh?'

Delia said nothing, but looked at him uncertainly. Yesterday someone had come into the room, and then discreetly withdrawn, while Kemal was kissing her, and she had it firmly fixed in her mind that the intruder had been Madame Renoir, a conviction that the little Frenchwoman's present attitude seemed to confirm.

She was probably putting quite the wrong interpretation on Kemal's being with her now and it was time the matter was made clear, even though it would not be an easy subject to raise. If Madame Renoir mentioned one word to anyone else about it she dreaded to think what Clifford, Kemal or Sadi Selim would have to say.

'I will leave you!' She blinked hastily back to reality when Kemal broke the silence. Bobbing that polite little bow in the direction of his aunt, he squeezed her hand. 'Tante Yvette!' Briefly his eyes held Delia's uncertain gaze, then he half smiled. '*Gene görüşelim, bebek,*' he murmured, and Delia flushed at the name he gave her.

She watched him go with mixed feelings. His departure was certainly a relief at the moment, but Madame Renoir could prove almost as embarrassing a companion if she mentioned that scene she had interrupted yesterday, and Delia suspected it was in her mind to do just that. She smiled at her warily. 'You—you don't have to stay with me, of course, *madame*,' she ventured. 'I don't really mind being on my own, in fact I can stand a little weight on my foot now and I thought I might walk a little way in the garden later.'

'Better that you rest it for a while longer,' Madame Renoir advised, 'I do not mind in the least talking to you, in fact I shall rather enjoy it! We will exchange confidences, eh, *ma chère*?'

'You're very kind!' Delia ignored the suggestion of a confidential chat, and hoped it would not become too confidential; she would have her say first and hope it would end there.

Madame Renoir waved her hands to deny kindness, her bright dark eyes watching her closely as she smiled. 'You would prefer the company of Kemal, huh?' she guessed, and leaned across to pat her hand. 'It is understandable, *ma chère*!'

Delia was faced with the most difficult conversation of her life and she had little or no idea how to begin. Her heart was hammering hard in her breast and she was convinced that she would be wasting her time trying to make Madame Renoir understand her position.

'*Madame*——' She hesitated, her fingers locking and unlocking in her lap as she looked down at them. 'I—I think you might have the wrong impression, the wrong idea about—about something you might have seen.'

Madame Renoir sighed deeply, pulling a wry face

to express her regret. 'So! You realised that someone came into the room, hmm? Oh, *ma chère*, not
for anything would I have intruded into such a
moment!'

'But, *madame*, it was nothing!'

The little Frenchwoman looked every bit as unbelieving as Delia feared she would, then she spread
her hands in a gesture of uncertainty and looked at
her for an explanation. 'I would not have called
such a moment nothing,' she said, and a hint of dis-
approval told Delia that she must now explain fully
or create another wrong impression.

'I mean,' she explained a little breathlessly, 'that
it wasn't—it wasn't what you might have thought,
madame. Kemal was—that is, I made Kemal angry
and he walked off and left me; we'd been arguing
and I said something that angered him even more,
and he walked off. Then—then I called him back
and said I was sorry.'

'And that was when he kissed you?' Madame
Renoir asked, and Delia nodded. 'So he forgave
you for angering him, he came back to you and
kissed you like that and you say it was nothing?'
She reached out and touched her cheek gently with
one hand. 'No wonder he calls you *bebek*,' she said
softly. 'You do not understand him, *ma petite*!'

'I understand what you're implying, *madame*,'
Delia told her, desperately seeking ways to convince her, 'but aren't you forgetting Suna Kozlu?'

The Turkish girl had come into her mind unbidden, but she was as convincing an argument as
any Delia could think of, and she saw Madame

Renoir frown. 'Suna Kozlu?' she asked. 'I do not understand how she can have anything to do with this matter.'

Delia's senses struggled with so many possibilities that she felt slightly dizzy and she looked at Madame Renoir in a daze of indecision. Perhaps she had been tactless, to say the least, in mentioning Suna Kozlu, but it was too late now and she must explain. 'I—I believe Kemal Bey is—friendly with her, isn't he?' she asked. 'I mean, Cli—someone saw them together only yesterday, and then she was here, and Kemal was at her house, I thought——'

'Delia!' Madame Renoir reached for her hands and squeezed them gently, reassuringly it seemed. 'Kemal has known Suna all his life, her father is a business partner of Sadi Selim. I do not say that at one time——' Her expressive hands lent meaning to the words she left unsaid. 'But Suna Kozlu is a dedicated woman, and dedicated women do not marry men like my Kemal—such men are not amenable to a wife who wishes to—how is it you say?—wear the trousers, hmm?'

Delia merely nodded. There seemed no point in asking what would happen if Suna Kozlu continued to seek Kemal's company as she had done of late. Probably no one would be really surprised if she found after all that marriage to Kemal Selim was more to her liking than a career, least of all Kemal.

CHAPTER SEVEN

IT was such a relief to be able to walk and, although her ankle still hurt a little, Delia revelled in being able to get about again. She could once more be useful on the dig too, for it was easy enough to stay sitting down while she made the entry of their finds. The progress that had been made in her absence amazed her and she could well understand Clifford's enthusiasm when he showed her the foundation of the temple, complete now and with the various parts of its structure laid roughly in place.

Sitting on the canvas stool beside an assortment of archaeological debris, she took a moment to watch Clifford as he worked with her uncle on reconstructing a beautiful carved capital before matching it to one of the columns. He was really quite good-looking in a studious sort of way, his delicate, rather schoolboyish features belying his twenty-six years.

There was a frown between his brows as he concentrated on his task, and Delia wondered if he really was as easily hurt as Kemal implied, by her rather off-hand manner towards him. He professed to being in love with her, but she could not help thinking that, should he ever be pressed to choose between staying with her or going off on some archaeological expedition, he would have no hesitation in following his hobby, no matter where it led him. It was doubtful if he regarded her as cruel, as Kemal did.

Kemal presented a different set of problems altogether, and she wished she could penetrate that cool, polite exterior and get to know the man behind it. Once or twice she had caught a glimpse of the depth of passion he was capable of, and she could still shiver at the violence of it. A man like Kemal would never be easy, for he would demand nothing less than the exclusive attention of any woman who loved him. The rewards of loving him would be great, but never something to be taken for granted, and she wondered if Suna Kozlu ever would consider it worthwhile.

Dismissing Suna Kozlu with an impatient shake of her head, she looked across at Clifford again. She had never really thought what answer she would give Clifford if he took his declared love for her to the next logical step and asked her to marry him, but now she considered it seriously for the first time.

Her uncle, she had no doubt, would consider it a good match and so would her parents, for they liked Clifford and approved of him. The only doubt was in her own mind and she was forced to admit not only that she was not in love with Clifford, but that she was much too close to being hopelessly in love with Kemal Selim.

She sighed deeply as she faced the fact at last, and sat with a rather sad and unhappy face, looking across at Clifford. Maybe it would be as well if he did ask her to marry him and then perhaps she would realise just how much she had to lose if she turned him down.

Lost in her own thoughts, she looked up swiftly,

startled by the shrubs in front of her parting suddenly, her breath caught in her throat when Kemal stepped from the scented mass of magnolias. The bushes closed behind him and he stood for a moment looking across at her.

He wore dark blue slacks and no jacket, and his cream shirt fitted closely across the broad golden chest showing a suggestion of dark hair where the top two buttons opened. It was a very informal mode of dress for him and Delia wondered if she had ever seen him look more breathtakingly attractive. There was a vigorous sensuality about him, a suggestion of virile force that was stunning at close quarters, and she could feel her whole being respond to him as he came the few feet across the clearing towards her.

A hasty glance over her shoulder revealed the fact that, while her uncle was still seemingly unaware of the newcomer, Clifford had spotted him soon enough and was already straightened up and frowning across at him. 'Am I interrupting your work?' Kemal asked, and she shook her head.

'No! No, not at all!' Again she glanced over her shoulder, a gesture that, she realised with a start, was purely defensive. Since her talk with Madame Renoir she had not been alone with him, and to be so now made her nervously uneasy. Not that they were alone, strictly speaking, not with her uncle nearby and with Clifford's disapproving gaze on them. 'Did you want to see my uncle?' she asked, but thought she knew the answer even before he shook his head.

'I wished to see you, *bebek*,' he told her, and Delia instinctively frowned over that annoying title he seemed determined to bestow on her.

'By all means,' she said, a gleam in her eyes, 'but please don't call me that—that name, Kemal Bey!'

'*Bebek?*' He repeated it softly and half smiled. 'You do not like it?'

'I dislike being referred to as a baby,' Delia insisted. 'It's not only—belittling, it simply isn't true!'

Kemal looked down at her for a few seconds in silence and she thought she detected a glint of mockery in his eyes for her objection. 'Do you wish to quarrel with me again?' he asked, and Delia stared at him, stunned to realise that she had brought them very close to quarrelling simply by being hypersensitive about a nickname.

'No, no, of course I don't.' She hastily swallowed her pride before trying to remedy the situation. 'I'm sorry,' she said, 'but—well, I just don't like being called a baby.'

'You would prefer that I called you Delia Hanim?' Kemal suggested, and she looked up at him steadily.

'Why not just plain Delia?' she asked, and wondered why he smiled and shook his head.

'Because it is not possible for you to be just plain anything,' he said quietly. 'But if you prefer it I will call you Delia.'

It was very hard to look at him suddenly without being afraid of what he might see in her eyes, so she got up from her stool and walked a few steps to where a feathery tamarisk stirred its pink blossoms in the gentle breeze. She could just see him from the corner of her eye and at first she caught her breath when she heard soft vague movements, then the pungent smell of Turkish tobacco tickled her nostrils and she realised he had lit a cigarette.

'You—you said you'd come to see me,' she reminded him in a small breathless voice. 'What can I do for you, Kemal Bey?'

'First, you can adopt the same informality with my name as I have with yours,' he told her, and Delia turned and looked at him for a moment.

Then her mouth softened into a smile that was echoed mischievously by a brightness in her green eyes. 'Very well,' she agreed with deceptive coolness, 'how can I help you, Kemal?'

He drew deeply at the long flat cigarette and the resultant cloud of blue smoke successfully concealed his features from her as he answered. 'Madame my aunt is visiting an old acquaintance this afternoon,' he told her. 'I am driving her into Antalya after lunch. I shall be free for several hours after that and I have decided to drive somewhere, perhaps into the hills where it is cooler. If you would care to accompany me, Delia, I will be pleased to have your company.'

The invitation sounded very stilted and formal after the last few minutes' conversation, but it took her so by surprise that for a moment Celia was too stunned to reply. She looked at him with wide, unbelieving eyes and shook her head slowly. 'Go with you?' she asked huskily, and Kemal raised a brow.

'You have driven alone with—your friend, have you not?' he asked, looking briefly across at Clifford. 'Is it not quite common practice in your free society for men and women to be together on such occasions?'

Delia swallowed hard, searching those dark unfathomable eyes for some clue to his motive for suggesting such an uncharacteristic arrangement. 'Yes, of course,' she agreed. 'I was—I was thinking more of your customs.'

'It is unlikely that we will be stopping anywhere that there are people about,' Kemal informed her coolly. 'There will be little chance of our being seen together.'

'I see!' She remembered his rendezvous with Suna Kozlu—he had not been so cautious then, and heaven knew who else besides Clifford had seen them together, but perhaps that did not bother him so much as being seen alone with a foreign girl. The force of her resentment for Suna Kozlu's privilege startled her and she made no attempt to wonder why.

Kemal was watching her with one brow arched, questioning her tone and her obvious resentment. 'Is there something wrong, Delia?' he asked gently.

'Nothing,' Delia denied a little breathlessly. 'But you aren't always so careful not to be seen alone with a woman, are you, Kemal?'

She saw the slight tensing of his long fingers holding the cigarette, that was all, but it was enough to make her regret having raised the matter and she already deplored her impulsiveness. 'You have the advantage of me,' he said coolly. 'Perhaps you will explain?'

'I heard——' She bit her lip anxiously and shrugged, as if it was of little consequence. 'It's just that you've been seen talking with Miss Kozlu, quite openly,' she told him, 'that's all.'

He was far less angry than she expected, in fact beyond that slight tightening of his long fingers he betrayed more curiosity than anger and the dark eyes speculated for a second or two on the source of her information. Then briefly he glanced across at Clifford again and his mouth curled derisively. 'Clifford Aitkin, am I not right?' he asked.

Delia too glanced across at Clifford and shook her head uneasily. 'It doesn't matter,' she said. 'It really doesn't matter.'

Kemal took the necessary few steps that brought him close beside her, his proximity making her catch her breath, then he reached out and cupped her face in one hand, turning her to face him. 'It seems to matter to you, Delia,' he said softly.

'No, no, of course it doesn't!' she denied, and despaired of her own weakness when she trembled like a leaf at the touch of a caressing finger on her cheek.

'You will come with me?'

Her hesitation was only brief, then she looked up at him with her green eyes shining. 'I'll come,' she said, then hastily avoided the gleam of satisfaction in his eyes.

'Ah!' Kemal said softly.

Madame Renoir made it obvious that she approved of Delia's going on with Kemal for a drive after they dropped her in Antalya. She spoke of it at lunch time and it was apparent that Clifford was prevented from voicing his objection only by his natural reticence, and possibly because he noticed that Sadi Selim too frowned briefly when it was mentioned.

All through the meal Delia bore Clifford's reproachful gaze and she escaped from the table thankfully when it was over. As she left the dining-salon Clifford was beside her, his hand under her arm and his head already bent towards her as if to impart his objections as discreetly as possible, but intent on stating them nevertheless.

He was allowed no more than a few words, however, before Sadi Selim caught up with them, politely inclining his head in apology, his fierce old eyes indicating unmistakably that he wished Clifford to be elsewhere, although he was much too courteous to make the suggestion verbal.

'You are happy to consent to this—journey with my grandson, Delia Hanim?' he asked, and Delia hesitated before she answered.

It seemed possible that the old man was going to try and persuade her that going anywhere alone with Kemal would not only jeopardise her own reputation but incur his disfavour too, and she wondered how she could insist without doing the latter at least. 'I'm quite happy about it, Sadi Bey,' she said, and looked at him steadily despite a certain natural wariness of the fierce old man. 'I—I hope you don't disapprove.'

Sadi Selim looked at Clifford again with that unmistakable meaning in his eyes, and this time Clifford had little option but to act upon it, for the professor was already standing by the open door waiting for him to join him.

'I'll see you later, Delia,' he murmured hastily, and glanced at Sadi Selim as if he would like to have said more. Then he gripped both Delia's hands in his own and squeezed them hard. 'Be careful, darling,' he whispered and, before Sadi Selim's politely averted eyes, bent his head and hurriedly kissed her.

Delia flushed, not because she had been kissed, but because Clifford had seen fit to make what she saw as a gesture of defiance in front of their host. He would guess the old man knew he did not approve of her going with Kemal, and he wanted him to think there were more grounds for his objection than there was. She would tell Clifford about it at their next meeting and make it quite clear that she did not like having him lay claim to her in that way when it was bound to convey the wrong impression.

Sadi Selim remained, to all appearance, politely untouched by it, and he opened the door of the salon, then stood courteously aside for her to precede him. 'I may be permitted to speak with you for a few moments, Delia Hanim?' he asked, as if she had every right to bar him from the rooms in his own house. 'Until my grandson and Madame come for you, perhaps?'

'Oh yes, of course!' Delia seated herself, at his

indication, in one of the armchairs near the windows, and the old man sat opposite her. She could not imagine what he had in mind to say or do, but from his manner he seemed neither angry nor unfriendly and she looked at him briefly from below concealing lids. 'You—you don't mind?' she ventured. 'If I go for this drive,' she added hastily, and Sadi Selim spread his dark hands in a gesture of resignation.

'I have learned that one must move with the times in this age of rapid change, Delia Hanim,' he told her gravely. 'To stay silent is not always to approve, but simply to yield to changes that one cannot prevent. I would only ask that you understand fully the implication of such a—venture in the minds of the traditionally-minded people of my country.'

It was a difficult moment and Delia tried hard to find an answer that would let the old man know how she appreciated his concern without giving him the impression that she meant to change her mind about going. 'I understand,' she said quietly, 'but thank you, Sadi Bey, I appreciate your concern for me.'

'You are the niece of an old friend and a guest in my house, Delia Hanim,' he murmured. 'Naturally I am concerned for you.'

If she insisted he would probably think her not only bold but uncaring about either her own position or Kemal's, but she could not give up the chance to go with Kemal, so she must do her best to make the old man understand. 'It's—it's very different in England, Sadi Bey,' she explained after a moment or two, and the old man listened politely. 'There no one would see anything wrong in my driving about with a man alone.'

The old man looked at her with his fierce dark eyes and for a moment she quaked inwardly, wondering if he would go so far as to actually forbid the outing. Suna Kozlu came uneasily into her own mind and she wondered if the Turkish girl was behind his objection.

'Kemal is Turkish and my grandson,' he reminded her, speaking in his slow pedantic English as if he chose his words with infinite care. 'He is unmarried and a man susceptible to a woman's beauty as any other. I would consider it a stain on my family's honour if you should—find yourself in a situation that is none of your choosing, Delia Hanim.' For a moment the fierceness gave way to a surprising gentleness as he looked at her, and the truth dawned on her at last—it was not so much tradition that he was concerned with but her own vulnerability where his grandson was concerned.

'I'll be perfectly safe, Sadi Bey,' she said softly. 'I know I will.'

The craggy, hawklike features gave way to a smile, albeit an anxious one. 'You are—forgive me, *hanim*—but a child, and I must be certain that you know what you are doing. Your uncle possibly does not see the danger, but I know my grandson and——' He spread his long dark hands helplessly. 'How can I blame him for behaving in the manner of his forebears?'

Delia would like to have leaned across and taken his hand, reassured him as she would have done her father, but it would have embarrassed Sadi Selim, so she simply smiled and shook her head. 'One advantage of living in our kind of society, Sadi Bey,' she told him, 'is that we learn to cope with that sort of situation quite naturally. As for Kemal Bey, I'm simply going for a drive in the country with a friend.'

'A friend?'

The sharp dark eyes questioned her use of the word, and she was forced to recognise that to a man like Sadi Selim the idea of platonic friendship between a man and a woman was not only incomprehensible but unacceptable. 'I hope we're friends,' she said, and for a moment almost convinced herself it was true. 'As I hope you and I are friends, Sadi Selim.'

He was far too courteous to disclaim it, but inclined his head and lightly touched his forehead with his fingers. 'I am honoured, *hanim*,' he murmured, and looked up with a certain air of resignation when Madame Renoir became audible coming across the hall talking in rapid and excitable French to Kemal—it was too late now for anyone to do anything to stop her from going, and she got to her feet as the door opened.

Madame Renoir insisted on taking the back seat in the car while Delia rode in front with Kemal, and she kept up a bright excited chatter of conversation all the way into Antalya. The friend she was to see was of very long standing and they had not met for some time, but, she insisted, it would have been boring for Delia to come with her, for their conversation would have meant nothing to her. Besides, she suggested as she got out of the car, it would be much more enjoyable for Delia to drive with Kemal into the mountains.

As they drove off, leaving his aunt at her friend's door, Kemal turned and smiled at her and she realised, perhaps for the first time, just how fond he was of the little Frenchwoman. It was one of the glimpses of gentleness about him that sometimes surprised her.

She had no idea where they were going, nor did she really care, for being with Kemal was all that seemed to matter at the moment and she looked around her as they sped through the changing countryside. Woods and orchards flew past, and little patches of wild flowers growing by the roadside while the inevitable streams of cool water came rushing down from the mountains on their way to the sea.

Little villages with their buildings straggling along both sides of the road, each one set in its plot of land, backed by the hills with their dark forests of oak and cedar, gave an impression of peace and lushness. The rather untidy buildings softened by their setting of orchards and fields, the lanes occasionally blocked by flocks of goats in the care of dark-eyed children with solemn little faces. There was so much to see and she tried not to miss anything.

They had been travelling for some time, neither saying very much at all, although Kemal explained things to her readily whenever she asked about something she did not recognise. She had scarcely noticed they were climbing, but suddenly they were in the cooler air of the mountains and before them, like a picture painted in soft new colours framed in craggy rocks, was a broad green meadow lushly shaded by feathery willows and cooled by the inescapable sound of swiftly running water. Far from being deserted, as Delia would have expected, the meadow was alive with people, the green grass dotted with an assortment of tents. While she still stared at it in disbelief Kemal stopped the car, near enough to give a good view of the assembly, but far enough away to be discreet.

Delia turned and looked at him, her curiosity plain in her eyes. 'What is it?' she asked. 'Where are we?'

'A *yayla*,' Kemal explained. 'The summer pasture of these people. They were once *yörüks*, nomadic people, and these *yaylas* are their traditional summer retreat.' He indicated the men, women and children gathered there with what appeared to be all their worldly possessions, including their animals. 'Most of these people are settled now in permanent homes,' he told her, 'but some of them still return each year to their *yayla*, it is their custom.'

'It's fascinating,' Delia declared. 'They're something like our Romanys, I imagine, but they have so much—more, they look so content!'

'It is a contented life,' Kemal agreed, 'although

it can be hard, but these people ask for little except to be allowed to follow their own way of life.' She was aware, even without turning, that the dark eyes were watching her as he spoke and the realisation sent a tingle of sensation along her spine. 'What more does a man need than a healthy and amenable wife, lusty sons and his own land to work?' he asked quietly.

Still Delia did not turn, but her pulses were hammering wildly at her temples as she looked out at the women of the camp, tending the wood fires, carrying water and great pots of food. Kemal, of course, would see it from the man's point of view, while she, after reflection, realised how much work would be involved in such an annual trek.

There were the children too, the sons that he set such store by, and the little girls who would probably move into the more emancipated world of modern Turkey but were just as likely to be doing as their mothers did now in a few years' time. Dark-eyed children, solemn, as all Turkish children seemed to be.

'It sounds ideal from a man's viewpoint,' she agreed, still not turning round. 'But I'm not sure I'd like being in the place of their womenfolk!'

The warm vibration against her own body, she realised suddenly, was Kemal's laughter and it was so unexpected that she turned swiftly in her seat and stared at him reproachfully without quite knowing why. His eyes glittered with a bright and slightly malicious amusement that challenged her to deny him the right to laugh at her.

'You see the women as—victims, Delia?' he asked softly, and shook his head without giving her time to reply. 'Did you not say yourself that they look contented?'

She was obliged to admit that, but she was still not convinced that it was not even more of a man's world among the *yörüks* than in the rest of Turkey. 'Maybe,' she allowed, 'but are they really as contented as they look? Do they have any say in who they marry, for instance?'

Again his eyes glittered with laughter and the strong whiteness of his teeth mocked her in that dark face. 'Are men and women any different because of more strict customs?' he asked. He looked across at the camp set amid the peaceful beauty of the mountain meadow and smiled slowly. 'Passions can run high here in these surroundings,' he told her, 'for the young people are less sternly guarded on the *yayla* and elopements are not unknown.'

'Elopements?' Delia stared at him, unsure whether to believe it was true or that he was making the whole thing up to convince her that it was more romantic than she thought.

'A boy will run off with the girl of his choice,' he said, 'if there is opposition to their marrying, it is not unknown, and of course after that there could be no opposition, particularly from the girl's parents. Kidnapping would be treated as a serious offence if the girl was unwilling, but——' his expressive shoulders conveyed it all, 'what more romantic introduction to marriage than to be carried off by the man you love?'

He was so close. That warm, vibrant body just touching her, its contact bringing a strange, breathless excitement that made her senses reel, and the arm along the back of the seat, the softness of his jacket sleeves smooth against her bare neck. To be talking about elopement and the passions of a nomadic people in such circumstances was dangerously evocative, and Delia hastily turned away again, her heart beating furiously hard.

'I—I suppose in a country with such strict codes of behaviour,' she ventured in a soft, unsteady voice, 'elopements are bound to happen.'

One long finger brushed lightly against her neck and lingered beside her cheek, and she suppressed a shiver only with difficulty. 'Do elopements not happen in England also?' Kemal asked, and she nodded. 'And do you not also have parents who disapprove of their daughter's choice of a husband?'

'Yes, of course, sometimes, but they don't do much about it, usually.' She half turned her head and looked at him obliquely from the corner of her eyes. 'In England a woman's judgment is usually considered as reliable as a man's,' she said, 'so elopements are few and far between.'

His mouth curved into a half smile and he touched her neck again with that long, evocative finger as he spoke. 'And you do not approve of them, hmm, *bebek*?'

'Kemal——'

'You do not approve of being called a baby either,' he guessed, and his laughter throbbed against her, setting her pulses racing out of control.

He put a hand under her chin, turning her round to face him, the dark, glittering eyes fixed steadily on her mouth, as if it fascinated him, and for a long moment he said nothing more, but studied her face.

The flushed cheeks and long thick lashes that half concealed her eyes, the soft, tremulous mouth with lips slightly parted as she coped with the breath-taking beat of her heart. Beyond them on the lush green *yayla*, the dark-skinned men and women still seemed oblivious of their presence, and yet, to Delia, she and Kemal were suddenly part of the same picture. Passions ran high on the *yayla*, Kemal had said, but here, in the sleek blackness of his car, passions were also running high, and she prayed for the strength to control them.

'Delia!' His mouth was only a breath away when he turned in his seat and she would have surrendered to her own irresistible desires readily enough if Clifford's bitter and envious words had not come, unbidden, into her mind just as Kemal's mouth sought hers. Instead she turned her head quickly from him and his lips merely brushed the warm smoothness of her neck.

The words he uttered were in Turkish, but they sounded more like surprise than anger and she wondered a little dazedly if he had ever before been so abruptly repulsed. Surprise was shortlived, however, and it was anger that lent strength to the fingers that suddenly held her jaw relentlessly tight in their grip. He forced her to turn and look at him again so that briefly she met the glittering fierceness of his eyes before she closed her own.

'Why?' he demanded in a voice harsh with passion. 'I have kissed you before, *kadin*, and you have not turned away your head—would you have me believe you disliked the experience?'

His contempt hurt more than she cared to admit and the warmth of his breath on her mouth sent a shuddering surge of excitement through her whole body, but she said nothing, not even in her own defence. She could not lie about her reaction to his kisses, but neither could she let herself be carried along on that same tide of excitement again. Sadi Selim had tried to warn her, and Clifford had made sure that she knew he was still seeing Suna Kozlu, but she had refused to listen to either of them.

She tried to turn her head away, as much afraid of her own weakness as of his strength, and put up a hand to try and free his hold on her. 'Let me go, Kemal!' she whispered. 'Please!'

'Not until you tell me what I have done to deserve such treatment!' he argued fiercely. 'Is it because you have listened too often to what Clifford Aitkin has told you?'

It was startling to realise just how much she hated Suna Kozlu at that moment, and she almost shrank from her own violent feelings, but it was true. Suna Kozlu could get so much closer to him because she was of his race, she understood the complexities of the Turkish male so much better than Delia could.

Clifford had suggested that Kemal felt himself entitled to more than one woman at a time, and perhaps, if he was right, Suna Kozlu could accept such a situation, but Delia's senses rebelled against it, however much she wanted to love Kemal. It hurt to think of him with anyone else and she simply was not capable of sharing him, even if it had been possible.

She was unaware at first of the tears that filled her eyes and glistened on her lashes before they rolled down her cheeks. It was only when Kemal's cruel grip on her eased and he bent his head suddenly and kissed her cheeks that she realised she was crying over what seemed like an unsolvable problem.

Kemal drew her gently into his arms, holding her close to the warm comfort of his chest. 'Delia, *bebek*!' His voice was deep and gentle against her ear, muffled in the softness of her hair, and he kissed the smooth skin of her neck gently as he held her. 'Have I been too harsh with you?' he murmured. 'Was I too demanding for the baby that you are, *küçük*?'

Delia said nothing, she simply clung to him with her eyes closed, unwilling to be brought back to earth, while he pressed his lips to her neck and throat and the soft smoothness of her shoulders. If she thought about anyone but Kemal it was only to dismiss them as unimportant, and she looked up at last and put her arm around his neck while he leaned over her, his body pushing her back against the car seat.

His mouth found hers and she closed her eyes, breathless and unresisting, when he moulded her to him as if she was no longer a separate body but part of his. She was breathing unevenly when he

145

raised his head at last and looked down at her, and he smiled, brushing back the little strands of red-gold hair from her forehead with one finger.

'I must be very gentle with you,' he whispered softly, and lightly touched her forehead with his lips. 'You are such a baby, my Delia, hmm?'

She shook her head, her eyes bright and glowing, but he took no notice at all of her denial. He kissed her again and that was all she cared about at the moment—nothing else seemed to matter.

The drive back to Antalya to collect Madame Renoir registered only vaguely in Delia's mind, for she could think of nothing but Kemal—Kemal and his gentleness with her. They said little as they sped back through the villages and the lush countryside, but their silence was one of contentment and Delia wondered if she had ever been happier.

If she faced the facts, her position now was very little changed from when they set out from Mavisu, but somehow the thought of Suna Kozlu seemed less disturbing to her now and she felt much more confident of her own situation. No word of love had passed between them, it was true, but surely Kemal would not have been so gently understanding if he did not feel something for her, and her own feelings were no longer in any doubt at all.

If Madame Renoir noticed anything different in their behaviour towards one another, she made no comment, although there was a bright glitter of speculation in her eyes when Kemal saw her into the back seat of the car, and she glanced from one to the other.

She reported at length on her visit with her old friend and once, as they listened to her excited narration, Kemal turned his head briefly and caught Delia's eye, a dark glitter of amusement sparkling in his eyes. Had he been one of her own countrymen, Delia felt sure, he would have winked —as it was she found it difficult not to laugh delightedly at the intimacy his glance suggested.

'Did you enjoy your drive, *mes enfants*?' she asked as they turned into the gates of Mavisu, and Delia answered unhesitatingly.

'Oh, it's been wonderful, *madame*!' she told her. 'The countryside is lovely and up there in the hills it was so cool, so wonderfully cool and peaceful!' She glanced at Kemal trying to recall the strange words he had introduced her to. 'Kemal showed me where the—the country people go in the summer, I can't remember the name. A beautiful meadow on a plateau called a——' again she looked at Kemal and laughed at her own attempt at pronunciation, 'a *yazla*, I think it was.'

'A *yayla*, *bebek*,' Kemal corrected her gently, and she laughed at the sheer pleasure of hearing him use the name she had once disliked so much.

'You visited the *yörük*?' Madame Renoir asked, surprisingly knowledgeable, and shook her head. 'What would your uncle say, *ma chère*, if he knew that you had been visiting with such people, huh?'

'I don't know,' Delia admitted with a laugh, 'but we didn't leave the car, *madame*, we just sat in there under some trees and watched for a while.'

147

'Ah!' She put almost as much satisfaction into the single syllable as Kemal did, and when the car drew up by the steps she accepted his help as she got out, then, with a swift, sly glance at Delia, hurried on into the house and left him to render the same service for Delia in his own good time.

Recognising it as a discreet withdrawal, Delia felt the colour in her cheeks when Kemal's strong fingers closed over her hand and straightening up she found herself in contact with that now familiar warm vibrance that made her legs suddenly weak. He did not let go her hand but raised it to his lips, twining his fingers in hers so that their palms were together.

After a moment Delia looked up at him, her green eyes shining in a way she could do nothing about, and no longer caring if he read what was in her heart. 'Thank you for a wonderful afternoon,' she whispered, and Kemal smiled.

'Thank *you*, *bebek*!' he said softly, and bent swiftly and kissed her mouth.

He turned and got into the car again, taking it round to where it was garaged, while Delia turned to go into the house. It was as she turned that she saw Clifford, walking towards her, a little way along the drive and striding out in nervous, angry strides, and she hesitated whether to stay and wait for him or to go in and delay the inevitable complaint.

Her mouth still tingled from Kemal's kiss and her hand from the strong touch of his fingers and she could not face an angry objection from Clifford at the moment, so she turned hurriedly and went into the house—straight up to her room. It was inevitable that Clifford would have seen Kemal kiss her, even possible that he had seen her own unconcealed delight in his company, and she sought more to prolong her own pleasure than to snub Clifford—she would come back to earth soon enough!

CHAPTER EIGHT

It was after breakfast the following morning that Professor Crompton took the unprecedented step of suggesting a quiet *tête-à-tête*, and Delia, suspecting that it in some way concerned her outing with Kemal, agreed somewhat reluctantly. It was possible that Sadi Selim had whispered a word of warning to his old friend, but Delia was more inclined to believe that Clifford had somehow managed to impress upon his rather unworldly mentor that situations were developing which he knew nothing about.

Out in the gardens there was a warm wind blowing in off the sea that stirred the scented trees into gentle life and wafted their perfumes around them in heady profusion. It was a heavenly morning and Delia could think of no better way to spend it than in Kemal's company, but her uncle had requested that she walk with him immediately after breakfast, and it would be not only unreasonable but difficult to refuse him.

Overhearing the request, Kemal had given her a small quizzical smile, but there was a warm glow in his eyes that caused a curling sensation in her stomach and compensated in part for the uncertainty she felt. Clifford, she vaguely noticed as they left the house, was standing around rather aimlessly in the hall and did not even look at her.

There had been no opportunity since their return yesterday to speak with either Kemal or Clifford alone, for conversation had been general after the evening meal and it was much too late by the time the small party broke up to do anything other than go to bed. Delia had slept well, but she thought she heard voices in her uncle's room just before she fell asleep and she had little doubt that this morning's request for a chat was in some way connected with that late-night consultation.

'You enjoyed your drive with Kemal Bey?' Professor Crompton asked, and Delia's heart gave a wild lurch of warning as she nodded her head.

'I enjoyed it very much,' she agreed, wary and on the defensive even before she knew what he had to say.

Professor Crompton rubbed an anxious hand over the back of his head, his forehead creased worriedly as he paced beside her. His thin, ascetic features suggested that he was hopelessly out of his depth and knew it, and Delia felt suddenly sorry for him. To a single man, middle-aged and unused to the vagaries of her sex, it must have been rather alarming for him to be suddenly made conscious of his avuncular responsibilities.

'Clifford was speaking to me last night,' he said after an uneasy silence. 'He seemed to think I should have a word with you, Delia.'

'I can't think why,' Delia said, and there was an edge on her voice that must have warned her uncle how she felt, for he looked even less at ease.

'It isn't easy for me, Delia,' he told her, and once more rubbed a nervous hand over his thinning grey hair. 'With your father and mother so far away I feel—I *know* I have the responsibility of your well-being, but it isn't easy and—well, frankly, my dear, I don't know how to begin.'

Delia shook her head to deny anyone's responsibility but her own, but she could not help feeling for her uncle in his dilemma. Clifford would have made it virtually impossible for him to ignore the matter. 'Uncle Arthur.' She put a delaying hand on his arm and came to a stop in the shade of one of the wide-spreading plane trees, perching herself on the edge of the low wall. 'I can guess why Clifford spoke to you the way he did,' she told him. 'He saw —he saw me come back with Kemal yesterday and I could tell he was angry from the look of him— that's why I didn't stop and speak to him. I didn't want to quarrel with him and he looked as if that was what he had in mind!'

'My dear!' Her uncle frowned at her worriedly, relieved at least to have the subject raised without having to do so himself but unhappy about her air

151

of defiance. 'Clifford was very upset when he saw you—kissing, or whatever it was you were doing, with Kemal Bey. Since you're going to marry him you should be more considerate of his feelings, Delia!'

Colour flushed her cheeks warmly and she curled her hands, angry at the idea of Clifford claiming such a thing when it had no foundation in fact. 'I haven't said I'll marry Clifford!' she declared, her voice not quite steady. 'In fact, Uncle Arthur, he hasn't even asked me to marry him!'

Professor Crompton shook his head vaguely, apparently seeing such fine points as trivialities. 'But it's understood, my dear, surely,' he argued. 'I thought it had been settled between you.'

'Good heavens, no!' Delia looked at him dazedly. He surely must have misunderstood somewhere along the line, for Clifford would never presume so much. 'I didn't even know how Clifford felt about me until a few days ago,' she told him. 'I can't think where you got the idea from that I've promised to marry him, Uncle Arthur.'

'Really?' He looked so completely confused that Delia once more felt sorry for him. 'I must have misunderstood,' he murmured, 'but I'm certain that he told me there was an understanding between you.'

'Definitely not!' Delia could be quite adamant about that and she knew that proclaiming it firmly and often was the only way to impress it upon her rather absentminded uncle. 'There's absolutely no understanding of any sort between Clifford and me,

Uncle Arthur!'

Professor Crompton was shaking his head slowly, his hand again rubbing agitatedly over the back of his head. 'Then I fear you have failed to make the fact sufficiently clear to Clifford,' he told her. 'He must be firmly convinced that he's engaged to you to have decided to tackle Kemal Bey this morning.' He frowned worriedly and clucked his tongue. 'I do hope he won't go so far as to make our position in Sadi Selim's house untenable!'

Delia heard nothing of the last sentence, his first words had so stunned her that she stared at him blankly for several seconds before she spoke. 'Tackle——' Her voice cracked in her throat and she swallowed hard. 'He's—he's going to tackle Kemal about—oh *no*! Oh, Uncle Arthur, he can't, he mustn't!'

'My dear child!' The professor patted her hand, disturbed by her agitation without being quite sure of its cause. 'Clifford thought perhaps a word of explanation about the situation between you——'

'But there's nothing to explain!' Delia cried in despair. 'He has no *right* to say anything to Kemal!' She got to her feet, her heart pounding so hard that it almost deafened her. 'I must stop him!'

'My dear, I fear you'll be too late,' Professor Crompton told her. 'Clifford was waiting in the hall to speak to Kemal Bey when we came out here.'

'And Kemal was there too!'

Delia sank down again on to the wall feeling utterly dejected. No wonder Clifford had not looked at her, but had hung about in the hall with that rather hangdog air, waiting until she had gone out of earshot before he warned Kemal that by taking her out he was stepping over the bounds of good behaviour.

She was close to tears, although she was unsure whether they were caused by anger or self-pity. Kemal, she felt almost sure, would believe Clifford if he told him they were engaged to be married, for he had carefully probed into the question himself on occasion, having seen the way Clifford put on that proprietorial air with her.

She should have made more earnest objections to it at the time, for Kemal would now believe that her protestations of there being nothing serious between her and Clifford had been made simply to fool him while she indulged in a little illicit romance with his more mature charms. He would be angry and unforgiving because he thought she had made a fool of him, and she could have wept openly at the thought of that.

She sat on the wall that surrounded the flower bed, looking small and despondent among the riot of roses and lilies that scented the warm air around her, and suddenly felt lost. She looked up at her uncle, her eyes large and suspiciously bright. 'Uncle Arthur,' she whispered huskily, 'what am I going to do?'

For a moment he said nothing, but simply looked at her in that vague, helpless way. Emotional crises of any sort were not only alien to him but embarrassing, and he knew nothing of the agonies of being in love. Eventually he reached out and put an arm around her shoulders, hugging her close for a moment. 'I can't help, my dear,' he confessed. 'I know so little about these things.' He patted her shoulder consolingly. 'It won't be easy breaking it to Clifford that you—that you don't intend to marry him after all, but if you are determined, my dear, then it will have to be done.'

Delia looked up at him in despair—even now she had failed to make him understand. 'I'm not concerned with Clifford,' she told him in a small flat voice. 'It's Kemal I want to convince.'

'Kemal?' He took a moment to follow her meaning, then realised suddenly what she was implying and shook his head urgently, for the first time looking as if he was sure of his fact. 'Oh, my dear child,' he said, 'if you mean that you nurture some kind of —attraction for Kemal Selim, please put it right out of your mind! He's a man of—of sophistication, a traditionalist like his grandfather and Turkish to the core! I have no doubt that in time he will marry, but it will be someone suitable, of whom Sadi Selim approves. To expect anything more of him than a mild flirtation would, in your case, be very misguided!'

Delia walked from the garden in a state of complete despondency, leaving her uncle to make his way down to the dig. He had probably meant to be kind, but his last words had hit her like a physical blow, even though she had had much the same suspicion in the back of her own mind ever since her first encounter with Kemal.

She could not face working with them this morning, so she made her way back to the house, thinking that the peace and quiet of her bedroom offered a kind of sanctuary at the moment. There was no one about when she went into the house, but when she was barely half way up the stairs the salon door opened and Kemal emerged.

Instinctively she turned when she saw him, her lips parted, ready to call out to him, to ask him to listen to her side of the story, but one look at his face was enough to tell her that he was in no mood for reasonable explanations. He strode across the hall, sparing her no more than one long narrow-eyed look that seared her like a flame and left her too stunned to move for several seconds.

Turning suddenly, she went on up to her room, too unhappy to care about anything at the moment except that Kemal had looked at her as if he thought her beneath contempt. It was obvious that Clifford had spared nothing in the telling of his version of their relationship and at that moment she hated Clifford more than anyone else in the world for taking things into his own hands.

Madame Renoir would be in sympathy, she felt sure, in fact she was the one ray of hope on Delia's gloomy horizon. The little Frenchwoman had made no secret of the fact that she would like to see something develop between her nephew and Delia, but Delia had no way of knowing whether her desire was for something more permanent than the mild flirtation her uncle had seen as the only possibility.

When she at last ventured from her room there

seemed to be no one about and she went downstairs slowly. She shivered involuntarily when she considered the prospect of meeting Kemal again and being snubbed, and she hurried from the stairs to the salon where she hoped to find Madame Renoir. She did not want to see anyone else at all, especially Clifford, for she did not trust herself to be even basically civilised to Clifford in the present circumstances.

She opened the door of the salon cautiously, then almost closed it again quickly. Madame Renoir was not there as she hoped, but Clifford stood by the open windows, his hands thrust into the pockets of the fawn slacks he wore with a blue shirt. He turned when she opened the door, swinging round quickly as if he suspected she would immediately leave again if he did not stop her.

'Delia!' He came across the room in long jerky strides, his schoolboyish features slightly flushed and a dark look of anxiety in his grey eyes. 'Please don't go,' he begged, correctly interpreting her hasty move. 'Please, Delia!' It was difficult not to weaken before such an appeal and she hesitated, her eyes showing signs of recent angry tears and looking dark and shadowed. 'You've seen the professor?' he asked, and she nodded jerkily.

Holding herself stiffly, she fought with a returning anger, and curled her hands into fists at her sides. 'I don't want to talk to you, Clifford,' she said in a small, tight voice. 'I—I don't trust myself to be polite to you!'

'But what I did, I did for you, Delia!' Clifford

had his hands on her arms and somehow the door of the salon was closed behind her; it was almost as if she was being swept along by something she could not control. 'Delia!' Encouraged by the fact that she had not angrily shaken him off, he drew her towards him and even attempted a smile, albeit a small and rather bitter one. 'You didn't expect me to stand by and see you hurt by that—that man, did you?' he asked.

'If you're talking about Kemal,' Delia said huskily, 'there was little danger of my being hurt until you interfered, now——' She shrugged helplessly and Clifford bent his head earnestly as he led her, unresisting, to the centre of the room.

'Oh, Delia darling, you *know* he'd have hurt you sooner or later,' Clifford insisted. 'You know it as well as you know that I love you, and I couldn't just stand by and let it happen!'

Delia fought with a surge of emotions that was almost frightening in its intensity. Anger for his lie to her uncle, bitterness that he had probably made it impossible for her ever to get close to Kemal again, and a fierce determination to let him know how she felt about Kemal. 'I love him!' she whispered huskily, her green eyes bright and glistening as she listened to her own words. 'I didn't *want* rescuing, Clifford—I was happy as I was!'

'Delia!'

His hands on her arms tightened their grip and she was reminded suddenly of the way Kemal had gripped her so tightly just before he realised she was crying and gently kissed away her tears. The reminder of how happy she had been then only made her more angry with Clifford and she shook herself free of him at last. 'Leave me alone, Clifford!'

She walked across to the open windows and looked out at the exotic, scented gardens, wondering suddenly how much longer she would be able to stay at Mavisu now that this had happened. She had grown to love the big, exotic house with its perfumed gardens above the sea, as she had grown to love the man who lived there, and neither would be easy to forget.

'Do you think he'll ever love you?' The long silence was broken at last by Clifford's flat, resentful voice and Delia did not reply. She did not really know the answer herself, but the illusion had been sweet before Clifford shattered it. 'Delia, please!' He came and stood behind her, although for the moment he did not touch her. 'You *know* nothing could have come of it,' he urged quietly and so convincingly that for a moment she almost allowed herself to admit it.

'What—what did you tell him?' she whispered, and Clifford hesitated. Then he put his hands to either side of her neck and his fingers were caressingly gentle, as was his voice when he answered her.

'I told him we were going to be married,' he said. 'I said that—appearances were deceptive, that you were sometimes a—a little headstrong. The surroundings here had gone to your head and——'

'You had no right!' She could imagine Kemal's opinion of her now. A flighty girl, excited by exotic surroundings and flattered by the attention of a more mature man, lying to him about Clifford because she knew he would never have taken her out otherwise.

'I thought I had the right!' Clifford argued, tight-lipped, and Delia shook her head.

'He was so angry,' she said in a small flat voice. The hurt of being snubbed was still there and she shook her head slowly.

'He was angry,' Clifford agreed, making no attempt to touch her again. 'He's a proud man and he disliked being told where he got off, but I told him the truth, Delia—you *would* have married me if Madame Renoir hadn't put other ideas into your head!'

Delia turned, her eyes bright with unshed tears and her usually soft mouth closed in a bitter tightness that was completely unfamiliar to him. 'I *wouldn't* have married you, Clifford,' she told him with harsh frankness, 'because I don't love you!'

'I see!'

She was sorry for him suddenly. Sorry she had been so hurtfully blunt and appalled to think that she could be so bitterly cruel to anyone, let alone Clifford whom she had always liked, even more than liked at times. 'Clifford—I'm sorry!'

She put out a hand to him, a gesture of appeal, but he shook his head slowly and one hand rubbed over the back of his head in a gesture that was familiar enough to be touching. 'I love you,' he said in a quiet, flat voice. 'I hoped that by putting Selim out of the picture I'd make you see sense and realise what's best for you, but you still can't see, can you, Delia?' The grey eyes had a hard glittery look that made her shiver suddenly. 'Can you still think that you meant any more to Kemal Selim than a—a brief seduction? A last fling before he settles down with that Turkish girl I saw him with? You're fooling yourself, Delia, and I hate to think what you're going to do when he tells you so himself!'

'No!' Her cry came from the heart, but she looked at him with the cold certainty that he was right showing starkly in her eyes, and Clifford reached for her swiftly, drawing her into his arms.

With her head on his shoulder she cried bitterly, and Clifford held her, one hand stroking the dishevelled softness of her red-gold hair below his chin. It was soothing and comforting and, although the hurt was still there, her weeping eventually subsided and she looked up at him uncertainly.

'Feeling better?' he asked, but Delia shook her head vaguely.

'I—I can't blame you too much because you meant it for the best,' she whispered huskily. 'I just wish you—I wish you hadn't made Kemal believe that I lied to him.'

'Lied to him?'

Delia nodded. 'I told him there was nothing between us, you and me, and now he'll think I deliberately lied to him.'

He shook his head, as if her reasoning still puzzled him. 'I couldn't let it go on any longer, darling,' he said softly, and kissed her gently. 'Now it's been ended and you'll see, you'll forget all about him once you get home to familiar surroundings.'

Delia said nothing, but one thing she knew for certain. Clifford was wrong about her forgetting Kemal once she got back home. She could never forget him—whatever happened she would go on loving him, however hopeless it seemed.

Delia did not put in an appearance at lunch time, she sent her apologies to their host and said that she had a headache and felt slightly unwell. It was a reasonable excuse and not entirely untrue, and she simply could not face the rest of the household at the moment, particularly Kemal.

Madame Renoir, suspecting that her nephew's sudden ill temper and Delia's absence from the lunch table were somehow connected, sought her out during the early afternoon and persuaded her to join her in the salon. Delia did so willingly enough, although she was on tenterhooks for fear Kemal should come in, and Madame Renoir noticed it.

'You are not truly unwell, are you, *ma chère*?' she asked, and Delia, curled up on one of the cushions close by, shook her head.

'Not really,' she confessed.

Madame Renoir reached out and lifted the unhappy face with one finger under her chin. Shaking her head, she clucked sympathetically, although there was a speculative, almost shrewd look in her dark eyes as she studied her tear-stained face. 'Kemal is so angry that his anger almost chokes him,' she observed quietly, 'and you, *ma chère*, look as if you have been weeping. I am bound to connect these two things, so I ask myself, why have these two foolish young people made each other so unhappy, huh?'

Delia did not answer at once, and Madame Renoir did not press her to. She simply sat beside her with a hint of kindly curiosity in her dark eyes as she watched her. 'I—I suppose it was bound to happen some time,' Delia ventured at last. 'Clifford simply *had* to say something, to make some move.'

'Clifford?' Madame Renoir frowned at this unexpected intrusion of a third party. 'Monsieur Aitkin is concerned in this—this upset?' she asked, and Delia nodded.

It would be a relief to talk to someone who would at least make some effort to understand how she felt, and she hugged her knees to her, resting her chin on her arms as she gazed at the sunshine outside while she unburdened. 'Clifford told Kemal that I was engaged to him,' she said.

'To Monsieur Aitkin? Oh, *mais non!*' A hand reached for hers and pressed it consolingly. 'But this is nonsense, *ma chère*, is it not?'

Delia shook her head firmly. 'Yes, of course it is,' she said. 'I wouldn't have gone with Kemal the way I did if I was engaged to anyone, and I certainly wouldn't have let him——' She stopped hastily, but there was no need to go on—Madame Renoir was nodding her head wisely.

'So——' she said, 'Kemal is foolish enough to

163

believe what a jealous man tells him and he is angry because——' The expressive dark eyes rolled meaningfully, but Delia was already denying it, her cheeks flushed.

'He's angry because he thinks I made a fool of him, *madame*,' she told her bitterly. 'I always insisted that there was nothing between me and Clifford and Kemal took my word for it. Now he's convinced that I was fooling him and he's angry because he thinks he's been taking out someone else's fiancée. I can't blame Kemal, although it hurts that—that he won't give me a chance to tell my side of it.'

'You have tried to tell him?' Madame Renoir asked, and Delia shrugged vaguely.

'I saw him before lunch,' she said, 'but he—he snubbed me in no uncertain way without giving me a chance to—to say anything.'

She was close to tears again when she thought about it, and Madame Renoir nodded sympathetically. 'Stubborn creature!' she declared firmly. 'You did not lie to him and he has no right to make you unhappy like this! You should tell him so, huh?' She cocked her head to one side and listened for a moment to someone moving out in the hall. 'Maybe you have the opportunity, *petite*,' she told her in a stage whisper. 'I think he is coming here!'

'Oh no, *madame*, please!'

Madame Renoir got up from her chair and waved her back to her cushion. 'Tut, *enfant*, you are able to deal with Kemal I am sure of it,' she said confidently. 'Be firm, *ma chère*, do not let him frighten

164

you, hmm?'

Such advice was more easily given than followed, Delia thought wildly as she sat there watching while Madame Renoir spoke to Kemal as he came in, successfully distracting him for as long as it took him to see her out and to close the door behind her. He did not see Delia until he turned and began to walk across the room, and she saw him hesitate, his dark eyes looking almost jet black below drawn brows.

For a moment she thought he was going to turn and walk out again, and she shivered at the idea of him disliking her company to that extent, but he came on after that brief hesitation. He could have ignored her, she supposed, but his upbringing would forbid such ill manners no matter what she had done, or he thought she had done.

Inclining his head towards her in that stiff, formal little bow she was once so familiar with, he strode across to where a box of cigarettes stood on one of the small tables, and taking one he lit it with strong, steady fingers. His fierce dark features were thrown into momentary relief by the flame of the lighter and briefly his eyes turned again in her direction.

'I apologise for the intrusion, *hanim*,' he said, and the cold formality of his voice using that very formal title again made her heart lurch sickeningly.

She got to her feet and stood for a moment holding her trembling hands together in front of her as she followed his tall figure across the room with her eyes. Then, remembering Madame Renoir's admonishment not to be frightened of him, she swallowed hard on the thudding beat of her heart that threatened to make her breathless before she could say anything.

'Kemal!' She had to speak quickly before he walked out again, but when he turned he looked so discouraging that her courage almost failed her. 'I—I want to explain,' she began huskily, and licked her suddenly dry lips anxiously. 'I must——'

'You have no need to explain,' Kemal interrupted harshly. 'Your—fiancé has explained all the facts to me, and I having nothing to say to you, *hanim*, except that I admire the courage of a man who is so willing to forgive you and so ready to marry you still after the lies you have told!'

'Oh no, I haven't, please!' Delia shook her head, trying not to cry like a baby, for he too must remember what had happened the last time she had done that when they were together. 'I—I didn't lie to you, Kemal, please believe me, it's all a mistake!'

The dark eyes stunned her with their look of contempt and she felt herself cold and empty as she looked at him hopelessly. It seemed that Clifford had been even more convincing than she feared and Kemal was ready to believe him all the way. 'The mistake was mine, *hanim*,' he said coldly. 'I had seen Clifford Aitkin several times behave as if he had the right to kiss you. My grandfather has seen you also accepting this man's kisses without objection—am I to believe that we were both mistaken?'

'But I told you——' Delia began.

'That he meant nothing to you!' Kemal finished harshly. 'And I, against the evidence of my own eyes, believed you, *hanim*!'

'But it's true,' Delia insisted desperately. 'He wasn't—he *isn't*! He's a—a friend, nothing more.'

'You still seek to justify your deceit,' Kemal told her, ruthlessly harsh. 'But a man does not speak with such frankness and authority about a woman, nor does he lay claim to her so forcefully in public unless he is very sure of his position, even in your free society! My grandfather was present when he made such a claim, *hanim*, he would not have been so rash had he not spoken with authority! You made a fool of me for your own purposes and I do not like it, nor do I enjoy being told in front of another that I have been seducing another man's fiancée!'

'Kemal!'

He inclined his head again in that chillingly formal bow and swept those glittering jet dark eyes over her in a swift survey that brought the colour to her cheeks. 'I wish you joy of your marriage, *hanim*!'

It was because Sadi Selim had been there to witness his humiliation at Clifford's hands that it had affected him so deeply, Delia realised, for the old man would be appalled to think that his grandson had so far defied their customs as to behave in the way Clifford suggested. He had been disturbed at the idea of Kemal taking her out at all, unaccompanied—that she was now shown to be the fiancée

167

of one of his house guests would shame him deeply.

She could sympathise with Kemal to some extent and understand the way he felt, but her own hurt was at least equal to his, although he probably did not realise it, and he refused to hear her out. 'You *must* hear my side of it,' she insisted urgently as he turned away again. 'It's the least you can do, instead of condemning me out of hand!'

For a moment she thought he might relent, it showed in a brief softening of that stern mouth, but then he shook his head firmly. 'What more can be said?' he asked quietly. 'Your uncle is as firmly convinced as your fiancé that this betrothal exists, so there seems little point in your continuing to deny it. It seems you are to marry Clifford Aitkin, *hanim*, whether you admit the fact or not at the moment!'

He turned swiftly and walked across the room, his dark head held arrogantly high and the lean, hard body tall and straight as a lance. He had his hand already on the door when Delia found breath enough to call out to him, and she did so from the depth of her own misery, to try and hurt him as she had been hurt.

'Just as you'll marry Suna Kozlu, whether you want to or not?' she cried in a voice that shivered across the big room unsteadily.

Kemal stopped in the doorway, one hand on the ornate gilt knob, and there was a tense, taut look about his broad shoulders and the set of his head. Then he turned slowly and looked at her, his eyes glittering. 'Never, *hanim*,' he said in a harsh flat voice. 'I do not lie about such things!'

He was gone and the door closed firmly behind him before Delia realised that she had just learned something which yesterday would have delighted her—today it merely added to her state of confusion.

CHAPTER NINE

DELIA had firmly made up her mind by the time she came downstairs the following morning that she would not be able to stay on at Mavisu, no matter if her uncle and Clifford had finished their work on the dig or not. As things were her position was impossible and could only get worse as far as she could see, also she felt so weepy that she was losing patience with herself. She had been awake for hours during the night and she had given a great deal of thought to her situation both with Kemal and with Clifford, and the best solution seemed to be her early departure for home.

Possessed of a normally healthy appetite, despite her present unhappiness, she did not see how she could go on avoiding mealtimes just because Kemal would be there too. It would be hard to ignore him, but she would endeavour to concentrate instead on talking to Madame Renoir who was, she felt, her only ally in a somewhat hostile camp.

Sadi Selim was certainly no less courteous towards her and it was probably no more than her imagination, but she sensed that he was a little less friendly and more formally reserved since yesterday. Clifford greeted her warmly enough, but even he gave the impression that he had not entirely forgotten her adamant insistence that she did not love him enough to marry him.

She carefully avoided looking at Kemal, although from the corner of her eye she was aware that he inclined his head in that stiffly formal bow when she came into the room. His coolness hurt more than she had anticipated and she decided there and then that the sooner she left for England the better, as it was unlikely that his attitude would change; he had made that quite clear yesterday.

Heaven knew what made her decide to break the news of her proposed return home to Madame Renoir before she had even mentioned it to her uncle, unless it was because she knew instinctively that her sympathies were with her. Madame Renoir's reaction was much as she should have anticipated, she looked both anxious and displeased and she frowned over the news darkly.

'Oh, *mais non, ma chère*,' she said in a voice that must have been audible to everyone in the room. 'You cannot mean to go yet!'

Delia glanced hastily at the head of the table to see what her host's reaction might be, but apart from a look of polite interest the fierce, dark features betrayed nothing. She turned again to Madame Renoir, anxious not to be misunderstood.

'*Madame*——' she begged, but was waved to silence by a plump, beringed hand.

'You must stay at least until your goddess's temple is completely uncovered,' Madame Renoir insisted. 'Is that not so, Monsieur le Professeur?'

She appealed to Professor Crompton, but he appeared, at the moment, to be unable to grasp the significance of her question, and he merely peered at them both shortsightedly. It was Clifford who answered instead, and his reaction was all to clear. 'Delia?' He looked at her with a frown drawing at his brows. 'You can't really mean you're going home now!'

Delia took a moment to answer. She wanted so much to look at Kemal, to see how he reacted to the news of her imminent departure, but she feared she might find only indifference, so she kept her eyes downcast, ostensibly spreading butter on a *simmit* before adding sticky, sweet jam to it.

'I decided last night,' she said as matter-of-factly as her voice would allow. 'I'm not really contributing very much to the excavation and I'm sure Uncle Arthur will thank heaven when he's free of the responsibility of me!' She laughed a little unsteadily and glanced at her uncle. 'Isn't that true, Uncle Arthur?'

Professor Crompton's rather vague eyes blinked at her for a moment, then he shook his head. 'I shall be quite happy about whatever you decide to do, my dear,' he told her. 'If you feel you want to go home then do so by all means, I shall put no obstacles in your way. It's been more than two months now since we came here and you're possibly homesick, hmm?' He peered at her shortsightedly. 'Well, it's understandable, my dear, you've never travelled a lot and I've no doubt you miss all your young friends!' He glanced at their host, his smile vaguely apologetic. 'I'm sure Sadi Bey understands your reasons.'

The old man at the head of the table inclined his head in that small polite bow, his bright dark eyes hooded with concealing lids as he looked down the table at her. 'I understand, of course, Delia Hanim,' he told her in his smooth, courteous voice. 'Our house will be less pleasurable without you, but we honour your reasons for wishing to leave.'

The flowery little speech was evidently meant to include his grandson, but Delia doubted if Kemal shared his sentiments and at the thought of never seeing him again she was appalled to find that she was once more close to tears. It had not even occurred to her uncle that the events of yesterday had anything to do with her decision to leave, and she could only marvel at his lack of perception.

Madame Renoir, on the other hand, was fully aware of her reasons and apparently meant to persuade her against it. 'Are you .truly homesick, *ma chère*?' she asked, pouring more coffee for them both. 'Or are you just—escaping, huh?' There was no mistaking her meaning, but this time her voice was pitched at a more discreet level and it was doubtful if even Clifford on the other side of her heard what was said, although he was trying to.

Delia bit her lip anxiously, afraid that she might

weaken and cry like a baby at any minute, then she shook her head firmly. 'I—I just want to go home, *madame,*' she whispered huskily, and Madame Renoir almost undermined her control by gently patting her hand.

'*Pauvre enfant!*' she sympathised. 'I will not allow this to go on!'

'Oh, *madame*, please!' Delia whispered the appeal urgently, fearful of what her champion might do in her anxiety to see justice done. 'Please don't —don't do anything—it's better if I go home! My uncle can drive me into Antalya to the airport, in the morning and I'll fly to Istanbul, then get a flight home from there.'

'Alone?' Madame Renoir made flying home alone sound like the worst fate in the world, and Delia noticed that she looked at her nephew when she said it. Unless she was reading the signs wrongly, Kemal was being blamed for the whole thing and, even in her present mood, Delia could not condone that.

'I'll be perfectly all right,' Delia insisted, anxious only to be away as soon as possible now that the idea had germinated into a near fact. She smiled, albeit a little wanly, and shook her head. 'I'm perfectly capable of taking care of myself, *madame*, honestly,' she said. 'I haven't led such a sheltered life that I'm an innocent abroad.'

'You are a very unhappy girl who should have someone to take care of her,' Madame Renoir insisted firmly, and once again she looked at Kemal when she spoke with a wealth of meaning in her bright dark eyes. It seemed not to occur to her that either Clifford or the professor might as easily be designated to the role of protector and her intention, to Delia at least, was obvious.

'Please don't worry about me,' Delia begged. 'I'll be all right!'

Madame Renoir pursed her lower lip doubtfully. 'But why must you go so soon, *ma chère?*' she asked. 'A few more days perhaps, hmm?'

She would probably never know how tempting it was to yield to the persuasion of a few more days, but Delia shook her head, her mind made up. 'It wouldn't do any good, *madame*,' she said in a small, unsteady voice. 'It's much better that I go now—in the morning.'

Madame Renoir shrugged her plump shoulders, resignedly it seemed. '*Eh bien, ma chère*,' she said, and once more looked across at Kemal. 'You may safely leave the arrangements to me, I will see that everything is to your liking.'

In no mood to argue with the suggestion and thankful to have someone more capable of coping with the Turkish switchboards, Delia nodded. 'Thank you, *madame*.' Kemal, she noticed bitterly, seemed to find his breakfast far more absorbing than the prospect of her departure, and she once more swallowed hard on threatening tears.

'I'm not going to argue with you, Clifford!' Delia was feeling too emotionally weary to cope with Clifford's pleadings and she turned her back on him deliberately, to shut out the sight of those appealing grey eyes.

'I hoped you'd stay for my sake,' Clifford told her, and she shook her head firmly.

'No, Clifford, I'm leaving—for my *own* sake! I don't care how selfish that sounds to you!'

She had packed her suitcases last night and this morning she had taken a last look around the lovely exotic and now familiar bedroom that had been hers for almost three months now. The gardens beyond the open windows of the salon filled the air with their familiar scents and she closed her eyes briefly on the heady sensation of so many mingled perfumes.

Beyond her sight at the moment, and on the perimeter of the gardens, was the temple among the trees where it was possible to stand among the heady delights of magnolias and tamarisk and see the lights of Antalya merging with the stars at night, and the big golden moon shining across an amethyst sea. No matter where she went in the future nowhere would ever compare with Mavisu, and nowhere would she find another Kemal Selim.

The temple of Artemis would be restored without her further help. *Her* goddess, Kemal had called it, and she had come to think of herself and the goddess of Mavisu as having some kind of affinity, although it was a vague one. Kemal—everything came back to Kemal, and she was forced to face in earnest now the prospect of leaving and knowing she would never see him again.

Once again, as had so often happened in the past twenty-four hours or so, the tears were very close to becoming uncontrollable and she hastily shook her head, brushing one hand across her eyes to clear the threatening haze.

The little dark blue dress she wore buttoned high at the neck had seemed the most suitable one for her mood this morning, although she knew that she looked rather too much like a schoolgirl in uniform wearing it, but she didn't really care how she looked. Tendrils of red-gold hair already escaped from the tidy brushing she had given it and added to an overall *gamin* look that was very touching in the circumstances. Even her green eyes looked bigger than usual in the solemnity of her face, their thick lashes drooping heavily because she had slept little last night.

Clifford reached out and gently touched the nape of her neck and she could do nothing about the shiver of sensation it caused. It would be useless to pretend that she suddenly found him abhorrent, it was simply that he could not compare with the image of Kemal that refused to be dimmed in her mind, even through the dark hours of the night.

Clifford was young and attractive and there was no doubt that he loved her—if only she had the sense to fall in love with Clifford everything would have been so much easier and she would not now be on her way home to England feeling so utterly hopeless and dejected.

She turned at last and looked at Clifford, her eyes still glistening with the threat of tears, no matter if her mouth smiled softly. 'I'm sorry, Clifford,' she said huskily. 'I—I wish it could have been different, but——' She shrugged helplessly.

'I'm sorry too,' Clifford said quietly. 'Sorry I've caused you so much unhappiness when all I wanted was for you not to be hurt.' He put one long thin hand to her face and gently stroked her cheek. 'I love you, Delia,' he whispered. 'Remember that, won't you?'

'I will.' She was bound to cry now, she thought, and, as the tears started to flow, Clifford leaned forward and kissed her mouth with infinite gentleness.

Outside in the hall she heard Madame Renoir's voice and thought she caught her uncle's name, but nothing more, and there followed the murmur of voices for several seconds, but she did not move. Then a hand was on the door and her heart missed a beat when she realised that the moment had actually come to leave, and she stood with her hands tightly curled, her head spinning with a thousand and one reasons she could suddenly think of for not going.

Then the door of the salon opened and Madame Renoir came in, small and dark and quite incredibly bright in the circumstances. 'Delia, *ma chère*,' she said with a hint of smile, 'the car is waiting for you.'

'Thank you, *madame*.' She did not stop to reason why her uncle had not come for her himself, but walked over to join her in the doorway on legs that seemed barely able to carry her. Turning in the doorway, she looked back at Clifford, hesitated, then shook her head. 'I—I'll see you again, Clifford,' she said, and he nodded without speaking.

There was no sign of Sadi Selim, but she had said her goodbyes to the old man just after breakfast and she had thought then that he seemed more like his former gentle self and less coolly reserved than he had seemed last night. She had not seen Kemal since dinner the evening before. He had breakfasted early, Madame Renoir had told her, and then gone out. She did not say where he had gone, but Delia felt an envious bitterness when she imagined him with Suna Kozlu.

Outside the sun was hot and bright and the scents of the garden, more heady than ever, wafted on the warm wind off the sea. Through her gathering tears Delia caught the glitter of a black shiny car body and the rich gleam of chrome, she did not see her uncle or anyone else at the wheel, but suddenly the hand under her arm as the car door opened was no longer Madame Renoir's plump soft one, but a strong dark masculine hand that defeated her instinctive attempt to step back out of its reach.

Kemal must have come out of the house behind them and it stunned her to suddenly find him there, his dark eyes looking down at her, deep and unfathomable below straight brows, and the powerful warmth and vigour of him just touching her as he urged her into the front seat of the car. She had wanted to see him again, just once, even though it would have been making it harder for her to leave, but the thought of him actually driving her to the airport, making sure she took off, seemed unbearably harsh and she looked at Madame

Renoir in mute appeal.

'My uncle,' she whispered huskily as that relentless hand almost pushed her into the seat. 'My uncle's taking me to the airport, he——'

'You are coming with me,' Kemal declared coolly, and closed the door while she was still shaking her head in bewilderment.

Too stunned to protest any more, it was only after he had started up the engine that she realised she had not even said goodbye to Madame Renoir and she turned hastily, brushing away the tears that still clung to her eyelashes. Kemal was already driving them along the curved driveway to the road and she caught only a glimpse of Madame Renoir's smooth smiling face before they turned round a bend and she was lost from view.

She chanced a brief, anxious glance at Kemal as they took to the road and detected a hint of smile on his mouth. Why he had chosen to take on her uncle's job of ferrying her to the airport, she had no idea, unless some deep hidden sense of cruelty drove him to hurt her even more deeply by showing how anxious he was to see her gone.

'Why?' she whispered huskily as they sped down the steep hill road towards Antalya. 'Why didn't you let my uncle bring me, Kemal?'

He did not turn his head but kept that stern, arrogant profile turned to her, the expression in his eyes hidden by hooded lids and the thick short lashes that fringed them. 'Do you not trust me to drive you to the airport?' he asked, and even at a time like this she noticed the absence of any kind of title, which was not customary in polite Turkish conversation.

'Yes, of course I do,' she said, and subsided again, unable to attempt another opening with so little encouragement.

It was when they passed the road indicated as the way to the airport that Delia's heart gave a sudden anxious skip and then began to beat so furiously hard in her breast that it almost deafened her. She glanced again at Kemal's dark profile and licked her dry lips anxiously. 'Where—where are you taking me?' she ventured, and once more saw the brief twitch of his mouth as it admitted to a ghost of a smile.

'You sound troubled,' he told her. 'You do not trust me after all, hmm?'

'Kemal——' She half turned in her seat now as they sped out into the countryside without pause, and still he did not turn his head.

'Trust me, *bebek*, hmm?'

He turned his head only briefly, but the brief glimpse of his eyes and that familiar, once despised nickname sent a deep, vibrant hope surging through her suddenly, a sensation she made no attempt to control, but relaxed in her seat and leaned back her head. Eyes closed, she breathed a fervent prayer that she was not going to be rudely awakened from this dreamlike situation too soon.

Nothing had been said for a long, long time, it seemed, but to Delia their silence now had a deeper meaning, an air of contentment that this same journey had brought her before. For all that Kemal had an air of compulsion about him, it was not the tenseness of anger that had possessed him ever since Clifford made his claim to her, and his present demeanour was one that her own senses responded to urgently.

The strong brown hands on the wheel controlled the big car almost automatically, muscular wrists emerging from the white shirt cuffs below a fawn jacket, and the open neck of the shirt exposed the tanned length of his neck and throat where that small pulse throbbed steadily in vulnerable contrast. She could, Delia felt sure, close her eyes and describe every feature of him without pause for thought.

They drove as they had before, through little isolated villages, houses set each in their fertile acres. Orchards, houses, goats, children; all recognisable from their last visit, and Delia's spirits soared when they headed up the mountain road towards the *yayla* of the *yörüks*. In her heart she had somehow known that they would come back there, and she turned and smiled at Kemal, her last shadow of doubt dispelled.

The *yayla* suddenly spread out before them, surprising her as it had last time by its unexpectedness, and when Kemal cut the engine of the car the silence was almost tangible. The voices of the people in the camp were audible as from a distance and the thin bleating of the goats fell shrill on the warm air.

Kemal turned in his seat and looked at her, and

Delia could do nothing to stop the warm colour that flooded into her cheeks when she met the look in those dark eyes. There was a glow there that stirred every fibre of her being, and when he leaned across and brushed his mouth against her parted lips she reached out to him instinctively, putting her arms round his neck and drawing him towards her. The weight of his body pressing her against the soft leather seat had a hard urgency that her own body responded to with a turbulence that would have startled her, had she given it any thought.

'Delia!'

His voice had a passionate harshness that set her pulses racing and she lifted her mouth to him eagerly. He kissed her with a fierce passion that left her breathless, then strong gentle hands opened the neck of the high buttoned dress and exposed her soft throat to his kisses, caressing her with a compelling ardour that deprived her of all resistance.

She lay in his arms at last, her hands still about his neck, caressing the smooth golden skin where the dark hair began, and her eyes were softly green, her mouth still tingling erotically from his kisses. Kemal studied her in silence for a while, his dark eyes glowing, then he kissed her mouth lightly, one hand smoothing back the wisps of red-gold hair from her forehead.

'You remember the customs of the *yörüks*, *bebek*?' he asked, and Delia frowned briefly over his meaning, then she laughed a little lightheadedly and shook her head.

'I don't think I remember anything except you,' she confessed, and Kemal shook his head at her in mock despair.

He glanced across at the camp where, for the moment, their presence was being politely ignored, possibly because they had parked some distance away and it was taken for granted that they wished to remain in their own company. Then he kissed her again with infinite gentleness and looked down at her seriously for a second before he spoke.

'Sometimes a young man will carry off the girl of his choice, do you not remember?' he asked in a deep, soft voice that played havoc with her already chaotic senses, and she nodded.

'Yes, I do remember,' she said. 'He carries off the girl and——'

'And when they have presumed to have been together for one night,' Kemal finished quietly, 'no one objects to their marrying, you remember?'

'I remember,' Delia agreed huskily, and caught her breath on the sudden erratic beating of her heart.

Kemal traced the shape of her mouth with one long finger, gently pulling down her lower lip before he kissed her. 'Your uncle, Clifford Aitkin and Sadi Selim, my grandfather, all think that I have driven you to the airport,' he confessed. 'Only Tante Yvette knows yet that I have carried you off, my love.'

'Kemal?' Delia looked at him for a moment, startled and not quite sure if she fully understood him. 'What—what will they think?' she asked, but already knew that whatever he had done she would go along willingly with it because she could not bear to be parted from him again.

Once more Kemal studied her for a moment before he answered her, his dark eyes deep and fathomless, then he bent his head and his mouth pressed warmly to the small throbbing pulse at the base of her throat. 'Do you love me, Delia?' he asked softly as he raised his head again, and he found his answer in her eyes and in the eager arms that drew his head down to her kiss. 'Tante Yvette told me the truth,' he said, moments later. 'I could have taken physical revenge on Clifford Aitkin for his lies, my anger was so strong, but instead I have carried you off, my love, in the manner of the *yörüks*!'

Delia searched his face, briefly anxious again. 'And no one knows where you are?' she asked, and Kemal nodded.

'No one save my aunt, and she will not betray me, I think.'

'But——' Delia looked at him uncertainly, 'surely when we go back——'

Kemal leaned more closely against her, pressing her back against the seat, his body so warm and vibrant that she shivered at the excitement it invoked in her. It was so difficult to think about anything at all when he was so close.

'Your uncle would like you to marry Clifford Aitkin,' he suggested, 'and Clifford himself is surely not in favour of your marrying anyone but himself, my beloved. My grandfather has a great affection for you and he will accept you into his family if he is honour bound to do so, though his choice would have been a Turkish girl.'

'Like Suna Kozlu,' Delia suggested, unable to restrain herself, and Kemal shook his head firmly.

'Not like Suna,' he denied firmly. 'She is too independent by far for the traditional Turkish taste. I love *you*, my beautiful Delia, and I mean to marry you even against the opposition of your uncle *and* my grandfather, so that I see myself in much the same position as one of those hot-blooded young *yörüks* who has been denied the girl he loves. I can let you go out of my life and do nothing about it, or I can make sure that the opposition is removed —the conclusion of the story is in your hands.'

Delia gazed at him for a second, wondering for the first time just how strong the opposition was to their love, then she looked out of the window briefly at the nomads' camp. 'So you—you kidnapped me?' she said, and played with the idea for a second or two.

Kemal's big right hand cupped her face, the thumb caressing her soft cheek in sensual persuasion. 'Or we have eloped, *bebek*,' he said softly. 'It depends upon you.'

'Does it?' She looked up at him, her eyes soft and glowing. 'Where do we go from here, Kemal?'

He searched her face for a moment, as if it was not quite the reply he expected. 'Tante Yvette has a friend with a house not far from here,' he told her. 'You will stay in her house tonight, my love.'

Delia's heart was thudding so hard she could scarcely breathe and she gazed at him for a moment, only half believing this could be happening to her. Then she ran the tip of her tongue nervously over parted lips. 'And you?' she whispered.

Kemal's eyes glowed darkly for a moment and she held her breath on his answer. Then he leaned down and kissed her mouth lightly, almost teasingly. 'I, my darling,' he told her softly, 'will be staying at the hotel in that last village we passed through—well away from temptation. Unless,' he added with a sudden wolfish smile, 'you wish to follow tradition to the letter?' His laughter mocked the sudden swift warmth that flooded her face and she pursed her bottom lip reproachfully. 'Now, my little temptress,' he demanded close to her ear as he held her close, 'have I kidnapped you? Shall I take you to the airport after all? Or have we eloped in the traditional way and you will marry me?'

Delia stirred contentedly in his arms, her voice muffled when she gave him her answer. 'I like to follow tradition,' she said.

A GREAT VALUE!

Almost 600 pages of pure entertainment for the unbelievable low price of only $1.95 per volume. A truly "Jumbo" read. Please see the last page for convenient Order Coupon.

Margaret Malcolm

The Master of Normanhurst (#1028)
Normanhurst was bound to bring heavy responsibilities. How foolish, Rilla reminded herself, to feel jealous of the very possessions Piers wanted to share with her.

The Man In Homespun (#1140)
Clive had prejudiced Caroline against Adam—but one thing was clear. Whether one liked or detested Adam, it was utterly impossible to ignore him!

Meadowsweet (#1164)
If she'd never gone to Watersmeet, never met Philippe, she would have married Keith. But once Rosamund found real love, nothing else was good enough.

Anne Durham

New Doctor At Northmoor (#1242)
Gwenny was the forgotten member of the family until she landed in hospital being treated by Doctor Mark Bayfield. The Kingslakes considered him an enemy!

Nurse Sally's Last Chance (#1281)
Sally knew she was in hot water—but young, hurt and misguided, she seemed unable to trust the one person who could have helped her.

Mann Of The Medical Wing (#1313)
She was young, elegant and attractive—but she wasn't the girl Dr. Maurice Mann had come to meet. She was a stranger, even to herself.

HARLEQUIN OMNIBUS

A Jumbo Read!!!

Elizabeth Hoy

Snare The Wild Heart (#992)
Eileen had resented Derry's intrusion to make a film of the island, but she realized now that times had changed and Inishbawn must change too!

The Faithless One (#1104)
Brian had called her love an interlude of springtime madness but Molly knew that her love for him would never quite be forgotten.

Be More Than Dreams (#1286)
Anne suddenly realized her love for Garth was more important that anything else in the world—but how could she overcome the barrier between them.

Roumelia Lane

House Of The Winds (#1262)
Laurie tricked Ryan Holt into taking her on safari despite his "no women" rule—but found it was only the first round she'd won!

A Summer To Love (#1290)
"A summer to love, a winter to get over it," Mark had once joked. But Stacey knew no winter would help her get over Mark.

Sea Of Zanj (#1338)
A change of scenery, a little sun, a chance for adventure—that's what Lee hoped for. Her new job didn't work out quite that way!

LOOK WHAT
YOU MAY BE MISSING

Listed below are the 26 Great Omnibus currently available
through **HARLEQUIN READER SERVICE**

Essie Summers #1
Bride in Flight (#933)
Meet on My Ground
(#1326)
Postscript To Yesterday
(#1119)

Jean S. MacLeod
The Wolf of Heimra
(#990)
Summer Island (#1314)
Slave Of The Wind
(#1339)

Eleanor Farnes
The Red Cliffs (#1335)
The Flight Of The Swan
(#1280)
Sister Of The
Housemaster (#975)

Isobel Chace
A Handful Of Silver
(#1306)
The Saffron Sky (#1250)
The Damask Rose
(#1334)

Joyce Dingwell #1
The Feel Of Silk (#1342)
A Taste For Love (#1229)
Will You Surrender
(#1179)

Sara Seale
Queen of Hearts (#1324)
Penny Plain (#1197)
Green Girl (#1045)

Mary Burchell #1
A Home For Joy (#1330)
Ward Of Lucifer (#1165)
The Broken Wing (#1100)

Susan Barrie
Marry A Stranger (#1034)
The Marriage Wheel
(#1311)
Rose In The Bud (#1168)

Violet Winspear #1
Palace of Peacocks
(#1318)
Beloved Tyrant (#1032)
Court of the Veils (#1267)

Jane Arbor
A Girl Named Smith
(#1000)
Kingfisher Tide (#950)
The Cypress Garden
(#1336)

Anne Weale
The Sea Waif (#1123)
The Feast Of Sara
(#1007)
Doctor In Malaya (#914)

Essie Summers #2
His Serene Miss Smith
(#1093)
The Master of Tawhai
(#910)
A Place Called Paradise
(#1156)

Catherine Airlie
Doctor Overboard (#979)
Nobody's Child (#1258)
A Wind Sighing (#1328)

Violet Winspear #2
Bride's Dilemma (#1008)
Tender is The Tyrant
(#1208)
The Dangerous Delight
(#1344)

Rosalind Brett
The Girl at White Drift
(#1101)
Winds of Enchantment
(#1176)
Brittle Bondage (#1319)

Kathryn Blair
Doctor Westland (#954)
Battle of Love (#1038)
Flowering Wilderness
(#1148)

Iris Danbury
Rendezvous in Lisbon
(#1178)
Doctor at Villa Ronda
(#1257)
Hotel Belvedere (#1331)

Mary Burchell #2
Take Me With You (#956)
The Heart Cannot Forget
(#1003)
Choose Which You Will
(#1029)

Amanda Doyle
A Change for Clancy
(#1085)
Play The Tune Softly
(#1116)
A Mist in Glen Torran
(#1308)

Rose Burghley
Man of Destiny (#960)
The Sweet Surrender
(#1023)
The Bay of Moonlight
(#1245)

Joyce Dingwell #2
The Timber Man (#917)
Project Sweetheart
(#964)
Greenfingers Farm
(#999)

Roumelia Lane
House of the Winds
(#1262)
A Summer to Love
(#1280)
Sea of Zanj (#1338)

Margaret Malcolm
The Master of
Normanhurst (#1028)
The Man in Homespun
(#1140)
Meadowsweet (#1164)

Elizabeth Hoy
Snare the Wild Heart
(#992)
The Faithless One
(#1104)
Be More Than Dreams
(#1286)

Anne Durham
New Doctor at
Northmoor (#1242)
Nurse Sally's Last
Chance (#1281)
Mann of the Medical
Wing (#1313)

Marjorie Norell
Nurse Madeline of Eden
Grove (#962)
Thank You, Nurse
Conway (#1097)
The Marriage of Doctor
Royle (#1177)

Harlequin Reader Service

ORDER FORM

MAIL COUPON TO ➤ Harlequin Reader Service,
M.P.O. Box 707,
Niagara Falls, New York 14302.

Canadian SEND Residents TO: ➤ Harlequin Reader Service,
Stratford, Ont. N5A 6W4

Harlequin Omnibus

Please check Volumes requested:

- ☐ Essie Summers 1
- ☐ Jean S. MacLeod
- ☐ Eleanor Farnes
- ☐ Susan Barrie
- ☐ Violet Winspear 1
- ☐ Isobel Chace
- ☐ Joyce Dingwell 1
- ☐ Jane Arbor
- ☐ Anne Weale

- ☐ Essie Summers 2
- ☐ Catherine Airlie
- ☐ Mary Burchell 1
- ☐ Sara Seale
- ☐ Violet Winspear 2
- ☐ Rosalind Brett
- ☐ Kathryn Blair
- ☐ Iris Danbury
- ☐ Mary Burchell 2

- ☐ Amanda Doyle
- ☐ Rose Burghley
- ☐ Elizabeth Hoy
- ☐ Roumelia Lane
- ☐ Margaret Malcolm
- ☐ Joyce Dingwell 2
- ☐ Anne Durham
- ☐ Marjorie Norell

Please send me by return mail the books which I have checked.
I am enclosing $1.95 for each book ordered.

Number of books ordered _____ @ $1.95 each = $ _____

Postage and Handling = .25

TOTAL $ _____

Name _____

Address _____

City _____

State/Prov. _____

Zip/Postal Code _____

VW 130 260